Ima A

The Death of the Ghost's Wife

A Haunted Highlands Mystery

Book

Darren loves his job as a tour guide to Edinburgh's haunted houses, yet he doesn't believe ghosts are real.

Maybe he should have kept his opinion to himself though, as he gets sacked following a spirited argument with a customer. When his misfortune continues with eviction from his flat, Darren agrees to look after his grandmother living in a small village on the west coast, while she recovers from a broken foot.

Caring for his granny has its challenges. Her cat runs for cover every time she practises the bagpipes, and she believes she's sharing her home with the ghost of Darren's long-dead grandfather.

Things get weirder when he starts a new job cleaning houses around Argyll, especially when the old man he meets in the garden of one of them turns out to be a ghost. A ghost who wants him to investigate the suspicious death of his wife.

A light-hearted mystery set in beautiful Scotland.

Author

Ima Ahorn loves Scotland and visited there many times. After spending a long holiday travelling up and down the coast, hiking the highlands and island-hopping in the Western Isles, she decided to share her love of the country and the people by writing a book set in Scotland. The Haunted Highlands cosy mystery series was born, taking you to some of Ima's favourite places in the Scottish Highlands and Islands while entertaining you with mysterious deaths, Scottish myth and (almost) authentic characters.

A HAUNTED HIGHLANDS MYSTERY

THE DEATH OF THE GHOST'S WIFE

IMA AHORN

Copyright © Andrea Kling and Andy Koppe, 2025

All rights reserved. No part of this book may be reproduced or transmitted in any form or by any means, electronic or mechanical, including photocopying, recording, or by any information storage and retrieval system, without the prior written permission of the publisher, except for brief excerpts in reviews or articles.

Copyright © for German Original: Andrea Kling, 2022
Original title: Tot mit Garten
Original author: Ima Ahorn

Translated by Andy Koppe

ISBN: 9798268281729

Independently published

Andrea Kling
Eisteichweg 12
2630 Ternitz
Austria

Cover design by Andrea Kling
Images: ©canva.com

To Catherine and Andy.
This wouldn't have happened without you.

CHAPTER 1

Eyes fixed on the pavement, he slowly walked down the street. It was impossible to tell what he was hoping to find, as the ground looked the same throughout: worn cobblestones, bordered on either side by a narrow strip of paving slabs. Nevertheless, he soon seemed to find what he was looking for. He stopped, hesitated, then crouched down, staring at a particular spot. He extended a hand, fingers spread, palm down.

"Somebody died here," he announced in an ominous voice.

His audience watched him silently, while the usual noises of a Saturday night on Edinburgh's Royal Mile rang out behind him: chatting tourists, laughing pub-goers, a bicycle rattling down the cobbles.

Darren wondered who his audience saw when they looked at him. A boyish twenty-two-year-old who had fun mocking tourists? Probably not. His boss made sure that all his guides had a serious but sinister demeanour. The long dark coat let people believe that they had an authentic gentleman from the eighteenth century as their tour guide. His carefully gelled-back auburn hair and his narrow, pale face did the rest.

Finally, somebody cleared their throat. Probably one of the German or English tourists. They were always the first to get impatient.

"Do you know who it was? What happened?" he asked.

Darren looked at the speaker. "I have no idea."

He stood up and looked around. His sombre expression fitted his role perfectly, as he explained, "People died all around us. Hunger, disease and violence claimed countless lives: men's, women's and children's. For a long time, Edinburgh's Old Town was one of the poorest and most terrible slums in Europe. As late as the seventeenth century, the plague still wiped out entire streets."

His audience nodded gravely. But Darren knew they hadn't come for a history lesson.

"Fortunately, I should say," he continued, suddenly grinning. His eyes sparkled with mischief as he saw the shocked faces of his audience. "Otherwise, neither you nor I would be here tonight. Because old Edinburgh is a dark and eerie place. A place full of ghosts and ghouls."

After that, they no longer looked shocked, but relieved and excited. Yes, that's what they were here for.

"Most of us walk around the city seeing old houses, people, pubs. But some can feel there is more. Some are sensitive to the supernatural, to the world of ghosts and to the lost souls who dwell here. I can't promise that you'll see ghosts tonight, but over the next hour I will lead you to some of the spookiest places in Edinburgh, so you can experience for yourself how the cold hand of dread brushes the back of your neck."

He looked around the group. His smile seemed to mock people who came to the city to see ghosts. But there was also a warning in his gaze. He had spent hours practising in front of a mirror until he had achieved the right mix of invitation and threat. Now that paid off. Tense and excited, full of anticipation yet also apprehension, people were hanging on his every word.

With a mocking smile, he invited them to follow him down the narrow alleyways and into the dark cellars of the Scottish capital.

When Darren finished his tour at Greyfriars Kirkyard an hour later, everyone was happy. Of course, not one of them had seen a ghost, but nobody had really expected to. Not on a public tour with more than twenty people. Nevertheless, some would later claim that they had sensed something. A dark presence that had reached for them in the gloomy cellar of the haunted house. Something sending icy chills down their spines. That was why his boss's ghost tours were among the best in the city.

Meanwhile, he had said goodbye to everyone. Some had asked him for advice: a good book about Scotland's haunted houses, a cosy pub for rounding off the evening, or what else there was to see in Edinburgh. Now he was leaning against an old gravestone, grinning contentedly and counting his tips. Not bad for an evening out of season.

The old lady had waited in the shadow of the caretaker's hut until everyone else had left. Now she was hesitantly approaching Darren. He recognised her as one of his group. From England, he believed, even though she had hardly spoken during the past hour. She seemed unsure, as if she didn't know where to start.

When she took an old photo from her handbag, he groaned inwardly. It wasn't the first time this happened. Remember what your boss said, he warned himself, before preparing to disappoint her. He didn't feel much sympathy. After all, if she still believed in ghosts in this day and age, she only had herself to blame if others laughed at her.

CHAPTER 2

Darren rolled his eyes and let his head sink against the sofa. "It wasn't my fault, Mum," he protested.

He closed his eyes and regretted answering her call in the first place. Then again, if he hadn't, she would have kept ringing until he either relented or threw the phone out the window.

"Paul told me you insulted a customer. That's why he sacked you," his mother said.

"Paul called you? You talk to him about me?"

Darren was of course aware that she knew his boss. After all, he had invited his mum to Edinburgh himself, when Paul had organised a ghost tour for the employees' families. An opportunity to showcase his company, his boss had said. But he hadn't expected them to get along quite that well. They had swapped phone numbers and met up a few times since. And apparently they had started talking about him, Darren.

His mother didn't reply.

Darren sighed. "I'd have told you that I lost the job. It really wasn't necessary for Paul to tell on me."

His mother still didn't say anything. He hoped she secretly agreed with him. Eventually she sighed. "You know, Paul and I—we did indeed talk about you. And you should know he appreciates you. He thinks you're intelligent, reliable and entertaining. Just what he wants for his ghost tours. If only you could control your temper a little better. What on earth possessed you?"

Darren huffed. "I like people. I just can't stand the nutters."

"And what did that lady do to make you judge her like that?"

"At first, she only asked about the various types of ghosts I'd mentioned on the tour, and whether I'd ever talked to one myself. She seemed to think that I'm a freakin' medium. Of course I made it quite clear what I thought of that. But no matter what I said, she just wouldn't stop. In the end, she even demanded that I talk to her dead husband. Who does she think I am? Gordon sodding Smith?"

"Well, you are showing people round Edinburgh's haunted houses, so it's not too much of a stretch to expect that you can see ghosts."

"Those tours are for tourists! Nothing but a bit of a show to give them the creeps. Nobody ever believes they'll see a real ghost on a tour like that. No more than on the ghost train at a funfair."

"Did she tell you that she is a member of the Ghost Club?"

"She might have mentioned something like that. But belonging to the oldest bunch of paranormal nutters in the world doesn't give her the right to pester me!"

"So, what did you say to her?"

Darren squirmed. He was aware he could have handled the situation more delicately. "I politely pointed out that all so-called mediums are frauds, that ghosts don't exist, and that she should consult a psychiatrist if she insists on seeing things."

"It didn't sound like that from Paul."

"Yes, well. Maybe I was a little bit more direct, but the old bat just wouldn't let it lie. Not even when I referred her to the works of James Randi and Benjamin Radford, which prove that all that parapsychological rubbish is just one big swindle."

"Right, so that's why she complained to Paul and VisitScotland. She also threatened to write a strongly worded article for the club magazine. Not to mention her angry letter to Haunted magazine. You realise that Paul gets nearly half your customers through their recommendations?"

"Yeah," Darren grumbled.

"By the way, Paul said that he didn't sack you just because of the old lady."

"He didn't?"

"He would have kept you on if it hadn't already been the third time you've snapped. The third time this year, and each time it was just because folk told you they believed in ghosts—is that true?"

Darren didn't reply. Paul was right, of course. He knew he got irritated too easily by the crackpots he inevitably met in his job.

"I always thought you loved all this paranormal stuff," his mother said. "I remember when you were little, you had shelves full of books about ghost sightings, monsters and aliens. Wasn't that the reason you moved to Edinburgh in the first place?"

"Yeah, maybe. I mean, it was fun when I was little. But I know better now."

"So why of all places do you work on ghost tours with an attitude like that?"

"Because I enjoy scaring the tourists. Well, most of the time."

His mother sighed. "Anyway, maybe there's a good side to this. I actually called because of something else. Your grandmother has broken her foot and needs help for a while."

Darren didn't reply.

"I thought you could go and look after her until she's better. Although of course she insists she doesn't need a carer."

"But, Mum!"

"You don't have anything better to do right now anyway. And your father is still in Florida."

Darren knew what she meant: that her ex-husband would rather lie on the beach with his new squeeze than look after his injured mother.

Darren sighed. "Okay, I'll catch a train tomorrow lunchtime."

"Tomorrow morning. I already told Erica you'd be there for lunch."

He gritted his teeth. "Alright then. Tomorrow morning. But only for one week. After that I'll have to look for a new job."

"Fine by me, sweetheart. Love you."

She hung up before he could reply. Darren grumpily stared at his phone. Not only had he just lost his job and found out that his boss talked about it to his mother instead of him, but now he had to look after his grandmother who lived in a small village out on the west coast.

Tarus sauntered into the room, holding a mug of coffee.

"Problems?"

Darren scowled at him. No doubt his flatmate and landlord had been eavesdropping from the kitchen. "You have no idea."

Tarus gave him a pitying look. "Poor Darren. Do you have to visit your sick granny in the dark woods? Shall I pack a cake and a bottle of wine for the old dear? And be careful you don't get lost out there."

"Eejit. You only say that because your own grandparents are currently staying at the French Riviera instead of their absurdly large Highland estate."

"Guilty as charged." Tarus smirked and his grey eyes twinkled with amusement. Then his look turned serious. "How long are you staying out in the sticks for?"

Darren shrugged. "A week? Two?"

"Could it be longer?"

"Hopefully not, but yeah, it's possible. Why do you ask?"

Tarus slumped into an armchair, avoiding his gaze. "It's Abigail," he said eventually. "She's been on at me for weeks about moving in together. If it was up to her, I'd have kicked you out a couple of months ago." He gave his friend a contrite look. "And as you won't need a place in Edinburgh for a while, you'll have plenty of time to find somewhere new."

Stunned, Darren stared at his pal.

"Of course, you can leave your stuff here until you find something," Tarus hastened to add.

"You're throwing me out? Now? When I've just lost my job?"

Tarus looked at him with a pained expression. "I'm sorry, man, but you knew you could only have the room for a while."

Darren grumbled. It was true. He should have started looking for a new place weeks ago. But without a steady income, that would be next to impossible. At least if he wanted to continue living in Edinburgh's Old Town.

"Yes, okay. I'll move out."

"Thanks, man." Tarus grinned with relief.

When Tarus had left, Darren threw himself face down on the sofa.

Tomorrow is the start of the rest of my life, he thought in frustration. No job, no home, and in a dump so remote that there are only two buses a day—if that.

Yippee.

CHAPTER 3

Shortly after seven the next morning, Darren arrived bleary-eyed at Waverley station. He would have preferred to take a later train, but if he wanted to get to Ganavan by lunchtime, he had no other choice. Edinburgh's central station sat in a hollow between the Old Town crowned by the Castle and the Georgian New Town. On this murky morning, it was so dark here that the streetlights were still on.

As it was Sunday, it was pretty quiet. Most tourists were still in bed and the commuter crowds wouldn't be flocking into town again until the next day. Darren was glad to find an empty compartment. He threw his backpack onto a seat and flopped down by the window. He clasped his coffee mug and closed his eyes.

A few minutes later a noise woke him from his slumber. A couple, apparently tourists, peeked into his compartment in search of a seat. When they saw his pale face and red-rimmed eyes, they apologised and took flight. Now they'll believe there are undead in Scotland, Darren thought. Not that he cared much.

He knew he looked terrible. After his mother's call and the eviction by Tarus he had drowned his misery in whisky.

At Glasgow Queen Street station Darren changed trains. It would still be more than three hours until he arrived at Oban on the west coast, but even that small town would be only an intermediate stop. From there he would have to take the bus to tiny Ganavan, where his grandmother lived. The one silver lining was that he could pick up a tasty crab sandwich from the Green Shack by the harbour while waiting for the bus. With her broken foot, it seemed unlikely Granny Erica would be cooking for him.

An almost impenetrable veil of rain hid the magnificent landscape of Loch Lomond and the Trossachs, through which the train route was snaking from Glasgow. Forests, moors and mountains could only occasionally be made out in grey outlines. The hardy sheep that farmers kept here had taken refuge in their shelters or stood huddled behind ancient drystone walls. Darren was fine with the gloomy view. At least it suited his mood.

He pondered whether he should call his now former boss. If he showed some remorse, he might get his job back at Haunted House Ghost Tours. On the other hand, Paul knew what an excellent employee Darren was. That he had sacked him just because some mad old bat had bad-mouthed him hit Darren pretty hard.

He decided to leave the world of haunted houses and scary legends behind for now. It was all bogus anyway. Even though he did enjoy tricking the tourists.

Meanwhile, the train had passed the small station of Dalmally. Through the rain, Darren could barely make out the ruins of Kilchurn Castle.

He thought about his family. When he was little, his parents had often taken him to the mountains, to old castles or to the seaside. Then his father had suddenly announced that he was moving out. His mother had thrown herself into her new job in Perth, and Darren had to spend the summer with his grandmother. The following autumn he had started at a new school in Perth, but it wasn't the same. He rarely saw his father, who by then had moved to the States, and his mother had less and less time for him.

Only his grandma was always happy to lend him an ear, no matter what new hobby he was into. Although he could imagine better ways to spend his time than in a tiny village on the west coast, it seemed fair that he had to be there for her now that he was an adult.

After passing Loch Etive and stopping in Connel, the train turned south. It wouldn't be long now.

Trudging after the other remaining passengers, Darren got off the train in Oban. This was the final stop. Despite having a population of less than ten thousand, the town was the biggest place for at least thirty miles. It also had a ferry terminal, so for many people Oban was just a brief stopover on their way to the islands off the west coast. Darren would have to change here too.

To get out of the wet and the wind, he hurried towards the waiting room of the station. He needed to find out when his bus would leave. He no longer fancied a visit to the Seafood Shack, but maybe he could pass the time with a beer in the Corryvreckan. On the other hand, it was still a bit early for a visit to the pub.

"Chubby Cheeks!"

The shout made Darren snap out of his thoughts. He heard two girls walking beside him giggle. The three of them craned their necks looking for the source of the shouting. Darren soon spotted a broad-shouldered old man, who towered half a head above the other travellers. He had a weather-beaten face, grey hair, and stubble on his chin. Even though he was likely older than his grandmother, he looked in good shape. He wore a chequered shirt under a dark blue rain jacket. To his horror, Darren realised that the old man was looking straight at him.

"Uncle Greg?" he asked incredulously. The girls must have noticed that the embarrassing nickname was referring to him and giggled again. Darren felt himself blushing. He quickly approached the old man and hissed, "You're not supposed to call me Chubby Cheeks. Especially not in public."

Greg just grinned.

"I hope you're not here for me," Darren said.

Greg Gudgeon wasn't really his uncle, but an old friend and neighbour of his grandmother. He had known Darren since he had been a wee lad visiting his granny.

Now he nodded. "Oh, aye. Your mum called me. She said you might need a lift to Ganavan."

He was still grinning, showing his perfect white teeth. Darren suspected they weren't his own, as Greg was well into his seventies. Still, his wolfish grin made him feel like Little Red Riding Hood on her way to visit her sick grandmother.

As you might expect from the fairytale wolf, Greg announced, "There was no need for you to come. I would have looked after Erica."

"Err, okay." Darren didn't know what else to say to that.

The two men looked at each other in silence while the other passengers slowly disappeared into the rain outside. Eventually Greg cleared his throat.

"That's yours?" he asked, pointing at Darren's bulging backpack.

Not waiting for a reply, he grabbed the heavy bag and slung it over his shoulder. Then he led Darren out to the car park where his old blue Ford Focus was waiting.

The drive through town didn't take long, as the rain had kept many people at home. Having joined the main street, they went along the waterfront, with Oban's only proper row of shops to their right. There wasn't much to see here on a rainy Sunday out of season. They soon left Oban and turned into the narrow coastal road to Ganavan.

"Are you still hunting ghosts, Chubby Cheeks?"

Darren sighed. "I do guided tours, not ghost hunts. And can't you finally stop calling me that?" It wasn't the first time they had this conversation.

"What? Chubby Cheeks? It's what your grandmother called you."

"Just the once. I was seven and a bit tubby."

"You were nine."

"So what? I didn't like it, and she never did it again. Besides, I'm an adult now. So please call me Darren."

"Whatever you say, Chubby Cheeks." Greg smirked. Darren shook his head in frustration. That was how it always went.

"So, how does your ghostbusting business work? When you're called to a haunted house, do you try to trap the lost souls, or do you drive them out with an exorcism?"

Darren exhaled. He knew there was no point in correcting Greg. Whether it was ghost tours or ghost hunting, it was all just nonsense to him. Darren decided he might as well play along. He grinned.

"It depends on what kind of ghost it is. Some just want me to guide them to the light. Then they pass to the other side on their own. For the rest I need harsher measures. If you became a ghost after your death, I'd trap you and put you in a jam jar. Maybe I'd need to split you between a few jars. You're quite a lump, after all, and a bit of ghost energy in a jar makes for a pretty night light."

Greg laughed. "Very good. As a poltergeist I'll need to remember to sabotage your vacuum cleaner first, so you can't trap me."

"Don't expect that to save you."

"Right, I'll better stay off the poltering then. I could keep a low profile and just haunt your grandmother's bedroom every now and then."

"And you think she'd put up with that?"

He thought about it. "Erica? Probably not."

Meanwhile, they had reached Ganavan. Grinning, Greg steered his Ford through the village. Not much had changed since Darren had last been here. The windows of the primary school were decorated with paper flowers and a few lunch guests' cars were parked outside the pub. There was also a red post van.

Darren grinned. "Do you get post on Sundays now? That's better than in Edinburgh."

"No!" Greg grumbled, scowling at the van.

"What's up? Don't you like getting such good service?"

"If only we did! This Birtwistle fella is a right nuisance."

"That's the postie? What's wrong with him?"

"He fancies himself a real charmer. He spends hours sitting in certain ladies' kitchens and rambles on about everything under the sun, yet he can't even be bothered to deliver my newspaper on time. I should cancel the subscription and just fetch it myself. That way at least I'd get it on the right day."

"You're not jealous, are you?" Darren smirked.

Greg shook his head grumpily and turned the car into a narrow side street. Moments later he pulled into the drive in front of his small bungalow.

His bad mood evaporated as soon as they arrived. He grabbed Darren's backpack from the boot. "I'll walk you over," he declared.

Of course, Darren thought. He'll deliver me like the catch of the day. I wonder what payment he expects.

Sighing, Darren followed the tenacious old man down the narrow street to his grandmother's cottage.

CHAPTER 4

A grey ball of fur whizzed past Greg and Darren and disappeared on the other side of the street. The cat flap that Darren's grandfather had installed into the door of the tiny croft house swung back and forth wildly.

"Baudrons?" Bewildered, Darren stared after the cat.

Greg had already raised his hand to knock on the door, but now he hesitated. A muted whine came from inside the house. It sounded like the wail of a distant banshee.

"Maybe I better leave you alone for now," Greg suddenly announced. He quickly put the backpack down, turned and hurried towards the street.

Before Greg was three steps from the door, the whining turned into the ear-splitting howling of bagpipes. Shaking his head, his steps quickened.

Darren was left behind on his own. There was no escape for him. The howling turned into a barely recognisable but lively version of 'Scotland the Brave'. Since knocking seemed pointless given the noise level, Darren simply opened the door and entered.

Grandmother Bagshaw's cottage only had two rooms. As there was no porch, he immediately found himself in the living room, which also served as the kitchen. The large wooden table with the uncomfortable bench and sturdy chairs still took up most of the room. Since his childhood, this was where everything important happened in Granny's home, be it cooking, eating or schoolwork.

Only an old armchair next to the stove and a rarely used sofa added a bit more homeliness.

As he had expected, Granny Erica was sitting in her favourite spot, the Orkney wicker chair with its high back that wrapped around the sides to keep out a draught. She was playing the bagpipes. As she recognised her grandson, the eyes of the petite woman lit up.

She let the mouthpiece drop and smiled. "There you are!" she called without interrupting the music. With a nod of her head, she motioned for him to put his heavy bag down. Then she picked up the mouthpiece again to fill up the air supply and finish the piece.

"I thought you were ill," Darren remarked after his grandmother had finished.

Granny Erica snorted with amusement and pointed at her leg, which was resting on a footstool. "I've broken my foot, not my mouth."

"And you thought now is exactly the right time to practise the bagpipes?"

She shrugged her shoulders. "Yes, of course. After all, I want to compete in the Highland Games again this summer."

"So it had nothing to do with Uncle Greg?"

Erica looked up at him with her big blue eyes. "How could you think something so absurd? I hope I didn't frighten him off!"

Darren smirked. "He was gone even faster than Baudrons."

"Thank God!" Granny Erica folded up the bagpipes and put them away behind her armchair. "Now I'll make us a nice cup of tea. I'm sure you're thirsty after your trip."

She awkwardly fished for the walking stick that was hanging off the armrest.

Darren immediately offered, "But I can do that!"

Erica beamed. "Thank you. Better make us some sandwiches as well while you're at it. I haven't had lunch yet, and you look hungry too."

Darren gritted his teeth. This is how it had worked since he was a boy. He would offer to do a small job, and his grandmother thought of half a dozen extra tasks for him. But of course he was here to help, he reminded himself.

He moved the kettle to the centre of the stove. While he waited for the water to boil, he spooned tea leaves into the teapot and placed two cups next to it.

"Aren't you going to warm the pot?" his grandmother enquired.

He stood with his back to her while he rolled his eyes. Nonetheless, he wordlessly shook the tea leaves from the pot back into the tin.

Then he put bread, cheese and a jar of chutney on the kitchen table. "Did you know I'd be arriving today? Mum was under the impression you didn't really want any help, so I thought she might not have said anything specific. I was surprised she told Greg."

Erica looked at her grandson thoughtfully. "Yes, I knew you were coming. I did tell her that I could do with your help. But not because of the foot. I can cope with that. I can do almost everything myself with the walking cast."

To prove it, she lifted herself out of her chair and limped to the cupboard to get out some biscuits. "No problem at all, see?"

Darren raised an eyebrow. His grandmother was seventy-two. He was glad that she was still quite healthy and could look after herself, especially as she had been living alone for fifteen years now. Nevertheless, he doubted that she was doing quite as well as she let on.

The kettle started whistling. Darren took it off the stove and poured some of the hot water into the teapot. He swilled it around the pot for a moment, then tipped the water down the sink. He spooned tea leaves into the warmed pot and filled it with hot water. His grandmother nodded contentedly as he put the result of his efforts on the table.

"You forgot the milk."

Darren sighed.

Having fetched the milk from the fridge, he joined her at the kitchen table. "What would you like my help with then? Do you want me to mow the lawn?" He wouldn't put it past her.

Surprised, his grandmother looked out of the window at her overgrown garden. Darren immediately regretted his cheeky remark because the grass stood knee-high between the ancient rose bushes.

"You think it needs mowing too? Maybe you're right, but that's not what you're here for. It's a matter concerning your grandfather."

"My grandfather?" Darren was surprised. "I didn't know that you still talked to the Kinsleys after what they said about my father."

Granny Erica shook her head impatiently. "I'm not talking about your mother's family. I mean your father's father."

"Grandpa Alan?" Darren looked at her curiously. "Have you finally found his pension papers? As the widow of a fisherman, you ought to be due something."

His grandmother shook her head again. "No. I don't expect anything from that anymore. What he paid into his pension scheme is lost. I don't want to argue with anyone about that again—no, your grandfather wants to talk to you."

Darren frowned. "Talk to me? What's that supposed to mean? He's been dead for fifteen years." He eyed his grandmother with concern. She might still be fit physically, but if she suddenly started talking to her late husband that didn't seem a good sign.

Granny Erica saw the look on her grandson's face and smiled uncertainly. "Maybe I should have listened to him. He said I shouldn't spring this on you straight away, but I thought you might have experience with it now that you're doing those ghost tours in Edinburgh."

"Experience with what?"

"With ghosts. Paranormal phenomena, if you will."

Darren sighed. "Are you saying you have talked to my dead grandfather's ghost?"

He looked around the daylit room as if he expected to see Grandpa Alan sitting on the threadbare sofa. In reality, he was trying to gauge how bad things were with his grandmother. The kitchen and the rest of the room were clean and tidy though. If she had delusions, at least they weren't affecting her housekeeping. Somewhat reassured, he turned back to his grandmother who was looking at him expectantly.

"So, can you see him?" she asked.

Darren shook his head. "Of course not. Ghosts don't exist." He eyed Granny Erica suspiciously. "Can you see him?"

"No." She sighed. "He only appears to me in dreams every now and then. He thinks you have the gift. At least that's what he told me."

"What gift? Being able to see him floating around here?"

His grandmother shrugged her shoulders and nodded.

Darren shook his head resolutely. "Ghosts do not exist. Just because I do ghost tours and have read a few books about paranormal phenomena doesn't mean I believe that nonsense. It's only a job. Or it was." He looked at his grandmother with sympathy. It had been a long time since he had last visited her. She must be lonely. Gently, he added, "I know you still miss him. But I'm not a medium and I don't believe they truly exist."

"I see." Granny Erica nodded curtly.

To lighten her mood, Darren changed the subject. He would worry about his grandmother's mental state later. "Anyway, what's wrong with Uncle Greg? Isn't he always helpful?"

His grandmother pulled a face. "He's wonderful when something needs fixing, but he's such a chatterbox sometimes. Once he's sat down with a cuppa at the kitchen table, it's impossible to get rid of him. It's as if his *bahookie* was glued to the chair."

Darren grinned when he heard his grandmother use the Scots word for backside. In Edinburgh he mostly spoke BBC English, so the foreign tourists could understand him. Listening to his Granny took him back to his childhood.

"It's better not to give him the opportunity in the first place," Granny Erica continued. "And it's not like I'm getting out the bagpipes every time he's around."

Darren spent the rest of the afternoon doing odd jobs around the cottage. Erica Bagshaw might say that she didn't need any help, but that didn't keep her from tasking her grandson with any work that needed doing. Under her beady eyes, he brushed cobwebs from corners, painted the window frame in the bathroom, and repaired a dripping tap. He wasn't naturally gifted with DIY talents, but the jobs he had to do while staying with his grandmother as a teenager had at least left him with some basic skills.

While he worked, Granny Erica entertained him with gossip about her neighbours.

To distract her from telling him even more about the love life of her friend Norma Widdicombe, he asked a question that had been bothering him for a while, "How did you manage to break your foot? You're not getting doddery, are you?"

Erica waved her hand dismissively. "No, no. Don't worry. It was just a wee accident."

Something in her tone made Darren suspicious. "And what exactly led to that little accident?"

Granny Erica sipped her tea. Eventually she sighed. "You'll hear the story anyway, so why not from me?"

Darren picked up his tea and looked at his grandmother attentively.

"Alright then. It happened during our preparations for the THG—the Tiny Highland Games. You might remember. Every year we organise something for the children in the village. It's almost like the real thing, with running competitions, tests of strength and a few events for the parents as well. A bit of fun for everyone."

Darren waved his hand impatiently to get his grandmother to continue and spare him the boring details.

"So we were on the green behind the school. There's plenty of space there and, as you know, it's got a marvellous view across the bay and the sea. The children had just finished their races and now it was the parents' turn. Welly throwing. You know what it's like—everyone has their own style. Some grab it by the leg while others hold the heel. The children had great fun cheering on their parents. Then it was Daisy's turn—you remember Daisy, don't you? Of course! She was in the same class as you. As usual, she took the matter rather too seriously."

Darren nodded slowly. Daisy's ambitiousness was infamous even during their school days.

"The nursery bairns were lined up like organ pipes along the side of the pitch. Daisy grabbed the welly with both hands and started spinning in circles to build up momentum. Once, twice, three times. She spun around faster and faster, until on the last spin the boot slipped from her fingers and flew inches over the heads of the children towards the headteacher. Luckily, Miss Lindsay was just about able to jump out of the way."

"But how did you break your foot in the process?"

"I'll get to that in a moment. So Miss Lindsay stumbles about and desperately tries to hold on to something, but where are the big strong Highlanders when you need one? The only thing nearby was the tent we'd put up for the girls to get changed for the dancing competition. The tent unfortunately collapsed under her considerable weight."

"I hope nobody was inside."

"Only the minister."

"The minister?"

Granny Erica nodded. She tried to look concerned but didn't quite manage it. "You wouldn't believe how that man can swear. Reverend McEges wanted to appear in great kilt for the wee ones, like Rob Roy or something. Unfortunately, he was just getting changed when the tent collapsed on him. As Miss Lindsay and Daisy pulled on the canvas to free him, they also got hold of the kilt—and uncovered an unforgettable view of his pale full moon." Erica giggled.

Darren smiled. Then he furrowed his brows. "Why wasn't he wearing underpants?"

His grandmother raised her hands, baffled. "He didn't say."

"So where do you fit into the story? Did a tent pole hit you or something?"

"God forbid," Granny Erica protested. "Luckily, I was standing just far enough away. I was supposed to accompany the dancing competition on the bagpipes. Otherwise, I wouldn't have been there in the first place. But at the sight of Reverend McEges's bahookie and his horrified face I laughed so hard that I stepped backwards into a rabbit hole."

"What?!"

"Nobody else was injured, by the way. Neither the children nor Miss Lindsay. Not even Reverend McEges, apart from his dignity of course."

Despite himself, Darren had to laugh. "That's typical Bagshaw—breaking your foot just watching! What did the others make of that?"

Granny Erica shrugged. "Not much really. I suppose Reverend McEges was grateful that my accident diverted everyone's attention from his impressive backside. However, word must have got around about it, as his next sermon was surprisingly well attended. Even though of course you can't see much under the cassock."

CHAPTER 5

Baudrons the cat reappeared in Granny Bagshaw's home in time for dinner. Soon afterwards, Erica retired to her bedroom.

Since the living room was the only other room in the tiny croft house, Darren would have to spend the night on the sofa, just like when he was a child. Baudrons, who usually slept there, made his displeasure known by sitting in the middle of the sofa and staring at him defiantly. To pacify the cat, Darren tickled Baudrons's tummy until he purred with pleasure.

It was still far too early for Darren to sleep. Back home in Edinburgh he would be meeting friends in a pub. Or he might watch videos on Tarus' giant TV until he couldn't keep his eyes open any longer.

But none of that was possible here in the miserable metropolis of Ganavan, Darren mused. His grandmother's old TV stood in a corner, unused and covered in dust. Even if she had a satellite dish, Darren doubted that the old cathode ray tube could still produce a picture. Switching on the radio wasn't really an option either. Even though his grandmother's eyesight was slowly fading, her hearing was still excellent. A radio playing in the room next door wouldn't make her happy, and one shouldn't wake a sleeping dragon.

An oppressive silence descended upon the house. Occasionally he heard quiet snoring from the other room or creaking in the old beams of the cottage. No wonder people made up scary stories in the olden days, he thought. Luckily, he didn't believe in ghosts. For a while, Darren listened to a weird scraping noise. It sounded like fingernails being dragged across a blackboard, but it probably was only a twig being pushed against the window by the wind.

When he couldn't bear it any longer, he dug out his headphones and slouched on the sofa, phone in hand. He was quite glad that Baudrons had settled down next to him. As long as the cat wasn't moving, everything should be fine.

Half an hour later, Darren put his phone away and fetched the bedding from the wardrobe. Finding a comfortable sleeping position proved difficult with his feline bedmate.

Eventually, Darren turned onto his back. With the armrest in his neck and Baudrons on his tummy he waited to fall asleep. It was always far too quiet out here in the countryside. Darren wondered how Granny Erica could sleep without the soothing noises of the city.

But the day had been long and exhausting. Soon his eyes lids grew heavy until he finally closed them and dozed off to Baudrons's purring.

When he woke some time later, it was completely silent. He felt chilly, yet for some reason he couldn't wrap himself further into his blanket. Slowly, a feeling of not being alone in the dark room crept up on him. It took him some effort to open his eyes and raise his head. His grandfather was sitting in the armchair where Granny Erica had sat earlier to play the bagpipes. Relieved that it wasn't a stranger who had sneaked in, he let his head sink back. Something bothered him about the presence of his grandad, but his tired brain couldn't quite grasp what it was. It wasn't that the old man was watching him. At least not just that.

Even though the room was darker than an undertaker's sense of humour, the figure in the chair was easily recognisable. Grandpa Alan wore an old Aran jumper and worn-out dungarees. He looked exactly like Darren remembered him, even though it must be nearly fifteen years now since he had last seen him. As a boy, Darren had been very attached to his grandfather, an avid fisherman, who still regularly went out to sea even though he was well past sixty. Until one day he didn't come back.

"What are you doing here?" Darren asked, rubbing his tired eyes.

Grandpa Alan smiled, his teeth glowing in the dark. "I live here."

Darren nodded dumbly and closed his eyes. When he had nearly fallen asleep again, he suddenly realised that his grandfather's answer made no sense. He jerked his eyes open, but his grandfather was still sitting in the armchair, smiling at him.

"Aren't you dead?" Darren asked. He wondered whether it was rude to point this out to his grandfather.

Grandpa Alan didn't seem bothered. "Aye, but I wanted to talk to you."

"I see." Darren still struggled to concentrate properly. He was so tired he could barely keep his eyes open. Every move, every turn of his head or lift of an arm, was as arduous as if he was stuck in treacle. Wearily, he closed his eyes.

"Is it better this way?"

Grandpa Alan's voice prompted Darren to open his eyes again. They were sitting on a dune by the sea now. The sun was out, and a few gulls and other seabirds were screeching in the wind. A gannet dived into the water not far from them. Their body shape allowed those birds to hit the water at sixty miles an hour and dive deeper and further than any other bird capable of flying, Darren remembered. His grandad had told him that at some point. They had found a dead gannet on the beach, and its size and pointed beak had greatly impressed wee Darren.

Confused, Darren squinted into the bright daylight. "How did you do that? How did we get here? Is this a dream?"

"Aye." The old man beside him chortled. "Of course it's a dream. Or did you think I'd scare you with a proper apparition on your first night?"

"Erm, I… I don't really believe in ghosts."

"I know, Erica told me. Which is why I thought it would be a waste of energy to manifest myself in your grandmother's home."

"Are you really a ghost?"

"Aye."

"Somehow I don't believe that. I think you are a dream I'm having because Granny Erica was talking about you."

"That's possible of course," the old man admitted. "But I also know you have some regrets about not believing in ghosts. What do you say to that?"

"Of course you know that. After all, you're a figment of my imagination."

Grandpa Alan scratched his stubbly chin. Darren could still remember the funny sound, which reminded him of Granny Erica's scrubbing brush.

"Hmm. Seems I need to think of something better to convince you. Or you could try to just accept you've inherited my gift."

"What gift?"

"Being able to see ghosts."

Darren stared at him doubtfully. "I'm sorry, but I simply don't believe it."

"We'll see," the old man muttered.

They looked out to sea together while Darren let his thoughts drift.

The next time he woke up, Darren knew it couldn't be a dream. His neck hurt where the armrest of the sofa was digging into it, and his arm sticking out from under the blanket was ice-cold. When he opened his eyes, he looked straight into the glowing eyes of Baudrons, who had settled on the backrest inches from his face, and who was studying him pensively. Darren huffed with irritation, but the cat was unimpressed and refused to move.

He briefly considered pushing the creature off the sofa, but instead he just pulled the blanket up over his shoulder and turned to the other side. He took a quick look at the Orkney chair, but even though it was still quite dark in the room, he saw it was empty. Grandpa Alan was nowhere to be seen. Relieved, Darren closed his eyes and fell asleep moments later.

He woke again to sounds of a fire being kindled in the oven. The poker banged against the grate and the oven door squeaked. He struggled to open his eyes. Outside it was only just dawn.

"Good morning, my boy. I didn't think you'd be awake this early," Granny Erica trilled.

Darren pulled the pillow over his head. It was still far too early for such a cheerful mood. A glance at the clock confirmed his suspicion—it was not even half past six.

An hour later, Darren dragged himself through the backdoor of the cottage to the bathroom. As his grandmother's home was so small, the bathroom was in an extension, which was only accessible from the outside. Fortunately, the entrance couldn't be seen from the street or the neighbouring houses, so Darren could risk venturing out the backdoor in his underpants and with sleep-tousled hair.

A little later he sat freshly showered at the breakfast table with his grandmother. He suspiciously sniffed the mug that Granny Erica had placed in front of him. It didn't seem to be tea.

"What is this?"

His grandmother raised her eyebrows in surprise. "Coffee. Did you prefer tea? I've also got herbal tea if you'd like something without caffeine."

He stared at her aghast. "I certainly don't want that!"

Darren cautiously sipped the coffee. Now that he knew what it was supposed to be, he could kind of taste it. A little bit anyway. Not much coffee powder, but plenty of milk. That's how his grandmother had always made coffee. Her strong tea definitely was better suited for his morning caffeine boost.

"Thanks," he mumbled. He resolved to make his own coffee from tomorrow. Maybe he could get hold of an espresso machine in Oban.

While chewing his toast, Darren pondered whether he should mention the dream about his grandfather, but he decided against it. His grandmother would only feel vindicated in her belief in ghosts, and he didn't want that. Besides, it probably was nothing more than his brain processing memories and the day's events in his sleep.

"Are you sulking?" Granny Erica looked at her grandson quizzically.

Confused, Darren looked at his grandmother standing beside him holding the teapot. "What? No! Why?"

Granny Erica raised a sceptical eyebrow. "I was just telling you that Norma and Janet are coming round this afternoon, and that it would be lovely if you could get some scones for us."

"No problem." Darren stirred his coffee absent-mindedly.

Erica put the teapot on the table and sat down across from Darren. "Something's up. If you were fine, you'd already have some excuse ready for why you can't be here this afternoon."

That was true. Darren had known his grandmother's friends Norma Widdicombe and Janet Fawkes for as long as he could remember. The pair sat at the kitchen table gossiping with his granny so often that the three of them could be mistaken for a coven of witches. Norma's throaty laugh only added to the impression. When they started making fun of their neighbours and friends, they were almost unbearable to listen to.

"So? What's up with you?"

Darren sighed. "Nothing. I'm just tired. Plus, I've just lost my job, my pal Tarus is throwing me out of his flat, and instead of looking for alternatives, I'm here."

His grandmother frowned. "If you'd rather go back to Edinburgh, don't let me stop you. I'll be fine."

"I didn't mean it like that. I'm happy to be here for you." Surprised, he realised that was the truth. He loved his grandmother, because she was the only one who'd always supported him. "I just don't know what I'm going to do after this."

"I see. Do you want to tell me about it?"

"Not much to tell really. It's just all coming at me at once. Even though I haven't done anything wrong. It was also totally unfair of Paul."

After Darren had told his story anyway, Erica looked at her grandson thoughtfully. "That wasn't the first time you ran into trouble, right? Weren't there also the esoteric bookshop, your parapsychology professor at university, and a couple other occasions? Why do you think you keep getting into arguments and can't hold down a job?"

"Well, it certainly isn't my fault! You can't blame me for having to deal with frauds and fools everywhere. Same again the other day. Even though no paranormal phenomenon has ever stood up to scientific scrutiny, some weird guy comes up to me and ominously announces 'I see dead people.'"

After that sentence, which he pronounced in a deep, creepy voice, he grinned at Granny Erica.

He waved his hands impatiently. "Oh, come on, Granny, I'm sure you know the film."

She shrugged her shoulders. "Is Sean Connery in it?"

Darren sighed. "Ah, forget it. So that bloke tried to persuade me he's a medium. He wanted me to advertise his services to our customers. As proof of his skills, he wanted to relay messages from my dead grandmother. How gullible did he think I am?"

Granny Erica grinned in disbelief. "But Alison Kinsley is still alive, isn't she?"

"That's exactly what I mean. Both my grandmothers are doing very well indeed. So why should I stay polite when confronted with such con artists?"

"Because it's part of your job? Or because your boss might have a different opinion to yours?"

Darren stared at her. "But that guy was a fraudster!"

"Fair enough. Nevertheless, you seem to act a bit like someone using a burning match to look for the light switch in a fireworks factory. Why did you have to work in an esoteric book shop if you think it's all nonsense? Why do ghost tours if you don't believe in them yourself?"

Darren shrugged his shoulders. "I am interested in supernatural phenomena. It's not my fault that so far nobody has been able to prove that ghosts exist. But maybe you're right, I should probably try something completely different."

"What do you have in mind?"

"I don't care. As long as I get paid for it, I'll do just about anything. After all, I can't live on your sofa forever."

Granny Erica nodded. "If you want, I could keep an ear out for you around here. Maybe someone in Oban is looking for a toothpaste squeezer," she said with a grin. "However, if you want my help, you need to pull yourself together. Stop stirring your mug like that—the tinkling is getting on my nerves. You'll sort out the scones for this afternoon please, and while you're in Oban, you could drop into Argyll Herbs and Teas to get me a bag of their wonderful evening tea."

CHAPTER 6

It took Granny Erica just a few days to find a job for him. Her friend Norma had a niece who was looking for an assistant. The interview—more like an informal get-to-know—was taking place at Granny Erica's home. It was a matter between friends, after all.

"So you're Darren."

At his grandmother's request, he had put on a proper shirt instead of the usual black T-shirt. His short auburn hair, which he usually wore artfully tousled, was neatly combed like that of a primary school pupil on his first day. Maybe that's why he felt like a piece of cattle at an auction under Libby Whatmough's scrutiny.

The estate agent didn't seem impressed. Maybe it was due to Darren's rather slight build and pale face. He certainly didn't fit her idea of a stoutly built handyman. According to her aunt, Libby was looking for kind of a janitor crossed with a cleaning fairy. Someone who would get the houses she was selling into decent shape for showing them to prospective house buyers.

"What experience have you got?"

Before he could even open his mouth, his grandmother jumped in.

"Darren can do everything: cleaning, repairs and gardening. I myself taught him how to do things properly. Besides, he's quite bright. I'm sure he'll do a good job."

Libby nodded. Apparently her aunt Norma had already told her something similar.

"Are you sure this job is for you though? Most of my other seasonal workers are foreigners. They're not afraid of hard work. They're just a bit superstitious sometimes."

She sceptically regarded his hands, which looked neither calloused nor particularly strong.

"It's just for this season," Granny Erica hastily interjected. "Until I'm back on my feet."

Libby nodded, but kept looking at Darren. Finally he felt obliged to say something. He shrugged his shoulders. "I'm sure I'll manage."

She nodded without much enthusiasm. "Alright. Let's give it a go. Do you have a car?"

Again Granny Erica didn't let him answer. "He can use mine. At least until I can drive again. That's why it's so important that his hours are flexible. You see, he has to take me to the doctor's and run errands whenever I need him to."

The estate agent sighed. "Okay. Pay is per assignment, and you can start tomorrow."

She scribbled an address on a piece of paper and slid it across the table. "Tomorrow at nine. Be there on time. You can pick up your contract from my office the day after."

When she was gone, Darren looked at his grandmother accusingly.

"I'm not a child. You could have let me speak for myself. Besides, I don't really want to work as a housemaid."

"Don't be silly. Libby is one of the most successful estate agents in the area. The pay is decent, and you can manage your time freely. If Norma hadn't convinced her of your qualities, you wouldn't even have got an interview with her."

Darren grumbled. "I'd rather have found a job myself. Behind the bar at Markie Dans or something."

The Markie Dans was a cosy pub in Oban. Whenever he was in Ganavan, he tried to spend at least one evening there. There was regular live music, the food was good, and it was popular with backpackers who stopped in Oban on their trips around Scotland. The girls were always happy to meet new people, particularly locals. No need to tell them that he usually lived in Edinburgh.

Granny Erica nodded. "I'm sure you'd love that. And they're probably just waiting for you there."

Darren shrugged. "Maybe not," he conceded. "But I still could have found a job at the Costa or at Café Shore." At least he wouldn't need to worry about his coffee supply there.

"But when would you have time for me then?" his grandmother asked.

"Before, obviously. Or after my shift." Darren sighed. "Okay, okay. I'm sure you're right, as usual. It's more sensible this way."

He imagined how his friend Tarus would laugh at the idea of Darren working as a cleaner. Housework wasn't exactly one of his favourite pastimes, as Tarus had found out soon after Darren had moved in. Fortunately, Tarus had enough money to employ a cleaner who sorted out the kitchen and their common living room once a week. It was only thanks to her that the piles of dirty dishes and old food packaging that Darren accumulated hadn't taken on a life of their own. He didn't know whether it was Tarus or the cleaning lady who had stuck a biohazard sign to the door of his room one day, but he couldn't deny that it might have been justified.

CHAPTER 7

The next morning, Darren got into his grandmother's little red Vauxhall Corsa and drove to the address Libby had given him. The place turned out to be an impressive Victorian villa. The old stone house was surrounded by a spacious garden and its patio had a wonderful view across Oban and the Sound of Mull.

"Unbelievable, right?"

Darren turned around in surprise. He hadn't heard anyone coming, but suddenly a girl stood behind him on the patio. She was tall, slim, and looked absolutely stunning. Darren's jaw dropped. Could this really be Victoria's Secret model Sandra Kubicka here in Oban? In any case, the blonde goddess looked like she could be the Polish supermodel's twin sister.

She grinned and mockingly raised one of her perfectly shaped eyebrows. "Finished gawping?"

Darren shut his mouth. "Erm, yeah. Sorry about that. I didn't think there was anyone else here."

She looked at him, waiting. After a few embarrassing seconds Darren's brain reported back for duty.

"My name is Darren, Darren Bagshaw. Libby, I mean Ms Whatmough, sent me. Because of the garden, I think. But if there's anything else I can do for you…?"

The beauty's grey eyes sparkled with amusement.

"That's lucky. There definitely is something I could use a little help with, *Darren*."

The enticing way she pronounced his name made him weak in the knees. "Of course."

She led him around the house, back to the drive. A blue Ford Ka was now parked behind his grandmother's Corsa. She opened the boot of her car.

"Come on, give me a hand."

She quickly got out a bucket full of cleaning utensils, a mop, and a pair of rubber gloves. "You can take the vacuum cleaner," she instructed him.

Darren stared at the mop, dumbfounded. "You're not the owner?"

She laughed. "Unfortunately not. I'm Margorzata Kozubowska. I work for Libby as well. I'm supposed to show you around." She offered her hand.

Still stunned, he took it. He nearly cried out at her firm handshake. Instead, he panted through gritted teeth, "Pleased to meet you, Margo…"

"Mar-gor-za-ta," she repeated slowly. "But you can call me Maggie".

"Maggie," Darren echoed and surreptitiously rubbed his aching hand.

The practical flat shoes, blue jeans and T-shirt still looked out of place on her gorgeous body, but at least they made sense now.

Still a bit dazed, Darren followed her inside the villa. He wondered why he was disappointed. He hadn't seriously expected to meet a supermodel here. And as her colleague—maybe he even had a chance with her.

While Maggie got an apron out of the bucket and pinned up her long blonde hair, Darren looked around the big, empty rooms of the ground floor in amazement. The entrance had a stone-tiled floor, with the rest of the house sporting expensive-looking wood flooring. The walls were painted in tasteful pastel tones, while the fireplace, the stuccoed ceilings and the banisters of the staircase leading to the upper floor were white.

"What is there to do in here?" Darren wondered. "It's all spotlessly clean already."

Maggie laughed. "Maybe for a normal home, but not for the people who can afford a place like this. Everything must be perfect here."

"You mean, like, with chocolate on the pillows?"

"Almost."

"So, what should I do?"

Maggie grinned. "You were saying you'd do the garden. Ever driven a ride-on lawnmower?"

During the next hour, Darren was busy bringing the garden up to scratch, while Maggie cleaned the ground floor windows. Unfortunately, Darren's work wasn't just whizzing around on the lawnmower. He also had to trim the borders, cut bushes into shape and weed the flowerpots. At least it was a whole lot better than cleaning toilets or whatever else needed doing inside the house. Especially as the weather was surprisingly mild for a spring day, which meant it was quite pleasant to work outside.

But whenever Darren thought he was finished, Maggie gave him a new task. Her eagle eyes didn't miss anything. Neither a sloppily trimmed border, nor the fat angel that must have fallen off its plinth during the winter. Two hours later when everything finally was done to her satisfaction, Darren sank wearily onto the steps at the entrance.

"We won't be taking a break until later," Maggie announced immediately. She put the cleaning bucket and the vacuum cleaner back in her car and took the apron off. "We still have to do the holiday homes before lunch."

Darren groaned. "Don't you have any pity?"

Maggie smirked. Then she batted her eyes.

"You're not going to give up already, are you, my strong young Highlander?" she purred. "I may only be a frail maiden, but I'm far from tired."

"I hate you," Darren muttered.

As he scrambled back onto his feet, Maggie blew him a kiss. "Very well, young hero. Mount your steed and follow me to our next quest."

Ten minutes later they reached their next workplace. After the Victorian villa, Darren was disappointed. The two adjoining holiday homes had a nice sea view, but they were so tiny that they couldn't contain more than a living room and a single bedroom each. At least that meant there would be less to clean.

Maggie handed him a key and pointed at the wooden cottage on the left. "You do that one, I'll do the other. We'll be finished in an hour and then we can have our lunch break."

Darren hesitated. "Don't I need any cleaning stuff?"

Maggie shook her head. "You'll find everything in the kitchen."

Then she remembered something else. She quickly dived into her car and emerged with a piece of paper, which she pressed into Darren's hand. "Here's what you need to do."

Aghast, Darren stared at the list, which covered a whole page. "How am I supposed to do all that in an hour?" he complained.

Maggie shrugged indifferently and put on her apron again. Before Darren had even finished reading the list, she had disappeared inside her cottage. He sighed.

Forty-five minutes later, his colleague announced that she was done. But instead of helping him, she took a deckchair from a storage box on the patio and lounged in the sun.

"Your work, your money," she replied when Darren grumbled about it. There wasn't much he could say to that, especially as she had let him have fun with the lawnmower at the previous job.

More than an hour later, he had got his cottage into a state that Maggie decided was just about acceptable. Dirty linen and towels had been deposited into the backseat of her car, and after he had vacuumed the living room for the third time, she was satisfied with that as well.

They got lunch from a take-away not far from the cottages and drove to a viewpoint nearby.

"How did you do that?" Darren asked after he had unwrapped his sandwich.

"What?"

"The cottage. How could you finish so quickly?"

"I'm just good at it," Maggie proclaimed confidently and took a bite of her prawn sandwich.

Darren looked at her doubtfully.

"You don't believe me?"

"Of course I believe you—but is there nothing else to it? No trick you'd like to share? I don't want to take twice as long as you every time. If you help me, you can have my muffin."

She eyed the chocolate muffin in his hand sceptically.

"I'm supposed to tell you my secret just for that?"

"Alright then. I'll buy you lunch for the rest of the week. With dessert. Even though I doubt so much sweet stuff will be good for you."

Maggie grinned and ran her hand over her flat tummy. "No worries. I can eat whatever I want. Good genes, you know?"

Darren nodded dreamily, eyes fixed on her shapely body.

"Hey!" Maggie's fist hitting his arm brought him back to reality.

"Sorry. You were going to tell me your secret."

"Okay. It's quite simple. That list I gave you. You don't always need to do everything on it."

Darren frowned. "That's what I tried to do, but you kept sending me back."

"Because you did it wrong. You can skip some tasks. Just not so that anyone notices, and you must never cut the same corners twice."

"So, if I don't hoover the hall this time, I must do it next time?"

Maggie shook her head. "Too obvious, the hall's usually full of dirty footprints. If they're still there afterwards, Libby will notice immediately. But if you haven't got enough time to polish the furniture properly, just give it a quick dusting and spray a bit of polish into the room to freshen up the smell. Just don't forget to do it next time."

"So you're only making sure that it looks like it's just been cleaned?"

Maggie grinned. "Exactly. Although of course I really do clean. Just not everything every time."

Darren nodded thoughtfully. "That makes sense."

"When you skimped earlier it was too obvious. That's why I had to send you back."

"How long have you been doing this for?" Darren asked.

"Do you mean my job with Ms Whatmough or working here in England?"

"Scotland," Darren corrected automatically.

Maggie rolled her eyes. "Scotland, England, it's all the same to me."

Darren sighed with resignation. Presumably lots of foreigners thought like Maggie, but that was no reason to allow her to insult him. "We're much better than them. That's why so many tourists come to Scotland."

Maggie laughed. "They come here because they fancy seeing some handsome, strong Highlanders. If you ask me, most leave rather disappointed. I mean, just look at you."

"Hey!"

"What? You must admit, you don't make much of a Highlander. And I didn't say you looked like Quasimodo." She smirked.

Darren pouted. Of course she was right, his charms lay elsewhere. Before the gorgeous Maggie turned him down outright, he preferred to steer the conversation back to his last question. "You were going to tell me how long you've been working here for?"

Maggie thought about it. "I've been in Scotland for four years now. It's my third season with Libby."

"Why are you here when you could be at home, married and with three lovely children?"

"There's more money here, and who knows, maybe one day one of the rich old geezers who buy those big houses will marry me. That's the plan anyway. You're welcome to drool a little for all I care, but I'm afraid you're too poor for me." She winked.

"Not too young?" he smirked.

"Hey! How old do you think I am?"

"Eighteen. Nineteen at most," he said with a straight face. "And of course, by too young, I mean too young for you to inherit my riches. Why else would a pretty young lady like you want a rich old geezer?"

Maggie grinned. "Nice save. Even though you laid it on a bit thick."

Darren grinned.

"And why are you here?" Maggie asked.

He shrugged. "I needed a job. I got into an argument with my last boss, and he sacked me."

"What did you do?"

"Ghost tours. You know. Showing tourists around supposedly haunted houses, telling them myths about poltergeists. That sort of stuff."

Maggie nodded thoughtfully. "I've been to a few haunted houses. Must be quite a scary job."

Darren shrugged. "Not really. It's all just show for the tourists. No real spooky apparitions."

"So you've never really seen a ghost?"

"Of course not." Darren grinned. "Have you?"

"No. Not the ghost. Only what he's been doing." Maggie shuddered.

"What's it been up to? Did it breathe cold air on your neck? Rattle its chains in the cellar?" Darren didn't even try to hide his sarcasm.

"No. Just leave dirty or wet footprints where nobody had been. Hide cleaning stuff. Things like that."

"So it was a poltergeist?"

"Quite possibly."

Darren grinned and shook his head in disbelief. "Are you sure it wasn't just someone playing tricks on you? So far nobody has ever seen a real ghost, you know. Poltergeists only exist in movies."

"You only say that because it hasn't happened to you. There's no way that what I saw was a trick!" Maggie replied heatedly.

"But ghosts don't exist. Have you never heard about Benjamin Radford? Or James Randi?"

She shook her head.

"They are scientists," Darren explained. "They investigated paranormal phenomena around the world. And you know what? None of them were real."

"But the ghost in the old church *is* real. I don't care if you think I'm crazy. I know what I felt." Maggie crossed her arms and stared at him defiantly. The chocolate muffin and the shared secrets were forgotten.

Darren withstood her angry stare for a while. Then he yielded. "If you say so."

Even though that wasn't an apology, Maggie seemed content and they finished their lunch in silence. Darren idly wondered whether he would mind if his girlfriend believed in ghosts. Not if she had a supermodel figure like Maggie, he concluded.

When they had finished eating, Darren looked across the sea to Kerrera. It seemed an eternity since he had last visited the island. There wasn't much to see there, but it would certainly be a nice break from cleaning. Suddenly, he wished he had the rest of the afternoon off. He could take the ferry to Kerrera or Mull and wander about a bit. Or he could just sit up here with a can of beer and look out to sea.

Soon Maggie started collecting the rubbish. Time to get going.

"What's next?" Darren asked listlessly.

Maggie didn't answer. When Darren looked up, her grey eyes sparkled defiantly.

"The haunted house."

Of course, what else? Darren sighed.

CHAPTER 8

The house certainly looked suitably strange. Even though it had been converted into a home, its original purpose as a church was still clearly recognisable. Maggie explained that the kitchen was in the former vestry. Walls and an intermediate floor had been added to divide the nave into rooms. Most of the stained-glass windows had been replaced with modern double glazing, except for a particularly beautiful one in the dining room, which often bathed the room in an eerie light.

"So this place is haunted?" asked Darren as they entered the house through the former side door.

Maggie didn't deign to reply although Darren was just curious whether there were any myths or stories about the old building.

Inside, the house looked surprisingly homely and modern. Light-coloured wood flooring and matching furniture prevented the old church from looking too gloomy. In the living room, several cosy armchairs were arranged in front of a large TV. The ceiling-high bookcase was well stocked, as if someone who loved reading lived here. A quick glance into the kitchen revealed that it too was fully equipped. There even was a steel monstrosity that Darren identified as an espresso machine.

"It doesn't look spooky at all," Darren said. "Apart from the frightening amount of money that someone must have put into it."

Maggie rolled her eyes and sighed. "I shouldn't have told you. But I think the house is creepy, and I'm not the only one. Ms Whatmough has sold it three times already. Each time the new owners moved out again after a few month. Now she's renting it out until she finds another buyer."

"Did the previous owners tell her why they didn't want to live here?" Darren asked curiously.

"Well, they didn't say it was haunted. Just that they didn't feel welcome. They spoke of things disappearing at inconvenient times. Car keys, socks, single shoes. Things like that. But they never claimed there was a ghost here—more likely a weird neighbour. Though if there is one, nobody has ever seen him."

"So that's why you believe there's an evil spirit here?" Darren scoffed.

Maggie stayed serious. "That's part of it. But I've also experienced a few weird things myself. Maybe there really is a restless soul here. Or perhaps the house is just cursed."

Darren shook his head in disbelief.

"Don't laugh! Curses are real. This church is ancient. I'm sure it has an aura, that developed over the centuries."

"You mean mould and decay?" Darren grinned. "I'm sure there's a simple explanation for everything that you or anyone else has experienced here. People lose things. There'll be draughts through the old stonework, and there could be bats living among the old beams in the roof."

"It's not that. There's a presence. And it's not friendly." Maggie shuddered. She really seemed completely convinced that this house was haunted.

Darren looked thoughtfully into her wide eyes. He would never have believed that the confident dream girl he had met this morning could be so gullible. On the other hand, he had met others like her on the ghost tours. It was always surprising how sober and intelligent people could fall for the cheapest tricks.

Darren shrugged. "If you say so. I certainly don't believe in ghosts."

"In that case you won't mind doing the upper floor." There was something funny about how Maggie said that.

"Of course not."

The rooms upstairs were furnished in the same modern style as the ground floor. There were four bedrooms of various sizes, a bathroom, and a storage room. Apart from the hall and the stairs, none of the rooms was particularly spooky or dark. The master bedroom had a large bay window, which had been cut into the outer wall at the gable end of the church. The other rooms had dormer windows. Those must have been added during the conversion, because Darren had never seen a church roof with dormers before. He couldn't sense any peculiar aura or malevolent spirit, just the air smelling a little musty, which was hardly surprising in an uninhabited house.

Darren opened the windows, gave the duvets a shake and plumped up the pillows. The rooms looked clean, apart from the slightly stale smell of rooms that had been closed for too long. A bit of dusting and some furniture polish should do the trick. Especially after the advice Maggie had given him at lunchtime.

Then he looked at the floor. Dirty footprints led from the stairs to every one of the four bedrooms. Not his own footprints, Darren noted with some relief. He sighed anyway. The whole upper floor was furnished with cream-coloured carpet. Maybe Maggie had thought up her ghost story just to get him to do the tedious job of vacuuming it all. Although in that case he had to admit she was an excellent actress.

Darren fetched an antiquated hoover from the storage room downstairs and started cleaning the carpet. It was hard work, but at least the heavy appliance was able to properly remove the earthy footprints. He had just finished the master bedroom and started on the next one, when the roaring of the hoover suddenly stopped. He looked at the ancient machine in frustration. Then he tried the power switch a few times, to no avail. Eventually he gave the appliance a kick, but that had no obvious effect either. Was its bag full? Or was there some other problem? He threw the hose on the floor and trudged down the stairs to look for Maggie.

He found her vigorously cleaning the stainless-steel fittings in the kitchen. When he had described the problem to her, she sighed and followed him upstairs. Once on the upper floor, she looked around warily, but whatever she was expecting obviously wasn't there.

Together they bent over the now-silent vacuum cleaner, but Maggie couldn't get the stubborn machine started either. A quick check of the dust bag showed that it was barely half full.

"A full bag wouldn't cause that anyway," she said.

"What else could it be?"

Maggie shrugged. "This thing is ancient. Maybe it just broke. Or it's the fuse. There are often problems with the electrics here."

"You want me to check?"

Maggie looked at him wide-eyed. "You're not going to leave me on my own up here, are you?"

Darren shrugged. "Why not? You don't really believe it's haunted up here, do you?"

She gave him a dark look and crossed her arms. "Say what you like, but I'm not staying here on my own."

Surprised, Darren noticed that she had goosebumps. "Fine by me. So what do you suggest?"

She thought about it for a moment. Then she walked over to the bedside table and pressed the switch of the lamp that stood there. It came on immediately.

"It's not the fuse," she concluded.

"So what now?"

"I don't know. I'm going back down to the kitchen."

She hurried down the stairs. As she passed the socket the vacuum cleaner was plugged into, she hesitated. She frowned and bent down. A moment later the hoover behind Darren started roaring.

Darren switched it off and followed Maggie to the socket. "How did you do that?"

She looked him straight in the eye. "I switched on the socket."

"But I'm sure I flicked the switch. After all, I'd already been vacuuming for a while," Darren protested. Then he looked at her reproachfully. "That was you."

Maggie shuddered and shook her head. "Why would I do something like that?"

"Because I didn't believe your ghost stories. And now you're trying to convince me that your 'evil spirit' has turned off the power." He used air quotes to mark the words 'evil spirit'.

Maggie glared at him. Then she shook her head and fled downstairs without further reply.

Darren stood next to the socket for a while and pondered. Why was it so important to Maggie that he believed her absurd ghost stories? Was it some kind of initiation ritual? Or was it because he'd been so insistent about not believing in ghosts? She certainly hadn't convinced him with her little prank. Of course she had switched off the socket.

Nevertheless, he admired her acting performance. When he had found her in the kitchen earlier, he could have sworn she hadn't left the room for the past half hour, and the goosebumps were pretty convincing too.

Either way, he would pay her back at an opportune moment. After making that resolution, Darren got on with the hoovering. There were no more problems of course.

Next, Darren tackled the furniture. He grabbed polish and a cloth from a cupboard in the bathroom and went to work.

The first piece was a beautiful old dresser in the master bedroom. He sprayed it generously with furniture polish and ran the cloth over the wood, but instead of going shiny, the surface turned matt. The cloth, which should have been gliding across it with ease, stuck to it.

Frowning, Darren touched the now rough and sticky surface. But even before he had a closer look at the spray can, he realised what had happened. The distinct smell hitting his nose wasn't furniture polish at all, it was hairspray.

He dropped the cloth and investigated the can more closely. There it was: someone had carefully placed a furniture polish label over the original one, so that on first sight it looked quite convincing. This certainly hadn't happened by chance. Somebody had deliberately played a trick on him.

"Maggie!"

Furious and with the bogus can of polish in his hand, he stomped down the stairs, but his colleague was nowhere to be seen. Neither in the hall nor in the kitchen.

"MAGGIE, you wicked witch! Where are you?"

He was just about to try one of the other rooms when he heard the front door. Then he saw his colleague, who had obviously just come in.

"Maggie!"

"No need to shout like that. What's up?" She looked at him expectantly.

"You tricked me with hairspray!"

"Hairspray? What are you talking about?"

"This! Admit that it was you!" He waved the can in her face.

She took the can off him and furrowed her brows while looking at the half-detached label. Then she sniffed it to be sure. "You are right. This is hairspray. Where did you get it from?"

"From the bathroom cupboard of course, where *you* put it. I sprayed the whole dresser with the stuff before I realised what it was."

"Seriously?" Maggie grinned. "That must have made quite a mess."

"It has. I hope you have nothing else planned for today because you'll have quite a job cleaning it off."

"What makes you think I'd do that?"

"Because you tricked me into using it!"

"I did not!"

"Yes, you did. And don't you dare give me that stupid nonsense about a poltergeist again!"

Maggie glared at him. "I have no idea what got into you, but I've had enough of you shouting at me. I'm finished down here. The key is in the kitchen. Have fun!"

With that, she stormed off. Darren heard the door slam shut. Shortly after, an engine started. He heard a noise behind him like someone sniggering. Darren spun around. Of course there was nobody there.

He looked at the can of hairspray he was still holding. I'll certainly not start believing in Maggie's ludicrous stories, he thought annoyed. Surely the sniggering was nothing more than the coffee machine gurgling in the kitchen.

He threw the can in the bin and grabbed proper furniture polish from the downstairs bathroom.

"So how do I clean that damn dresser now?" he muttered. After a few moments of indecision, he pulled out his phone and typed into the search bar. "There you go. Water and washing-up liquid."

When Darren had finally finished cleaning the dresser and polishing all the furniture, he breathed a sigh of relief. If this hadn't been his first day at his new job, he would have long since chucked it in. But he didn't want to risk his grandmother's wrath.

He went to the bathroom to put away the last of the cleaning stuff. Suddenly the door behind him slammed shut. Darren nearly hit his head on the sink from the shock.

It was weird, but since Maggie had gone, he felt like he was being watched. Maybe it was because it was so quiet. But now that the sun was slowly setting and the rooms were getting dark, the house really did feel a bit creepy. Obviously, it had nothing to do with it being haunted though. There are no ghosts, Darren reminded himself. It wasn't a poltergeist that had slammed the door—it had simply been blown shut by a draught because the bedroom windows were open. He was nearly finished anyway. He would just close the windows and head off.

Darren grinned. Maggie and her ghost stories.

When he reached for the door handle and pulled, he felt his fingertips sink into something soft on the underside of the handle. Shocked and disgusted, he tore his hand away. The handle came off the door and clattered onto the tiled floor.

Maggie! Darren cursed. He looked at his fingers to find an opaque, brownish substance. He sniffed it suspiciously. It took a moment or two until he could place the smell. Then he sighed, somewhat relieved. Shoe polish. Brown shoe polish. He had feared worse.

By now he was really getting annoyed. What was Maggie thinking? That he'd believe this cheap trick was played by a poltergeist? Had she never been on a school trip?

He went to the sink and turned on the hot tap until it was steaming. He carefully picked up the door handle and pushed it under the tap. Then, he washed his hands.

When he looked up, he flinched. There was a message on the steamed-up mirror. Yet even more creepy was the shadowy figure that seemed to stand right behind him in the foggy reflection of the bathroom. He spun around.

Of course, there was no one there. Gurgling laughter sent shivers down his spine. This time it definitely was not the coffee machine.

It's just the old pipes, Darren tried to reassure himself. He had another look around the bathroom before he turned back towards the sink.

"BOO!" it said on the mirror. Not a terribly original message for a ghost. Besides, it was easy to create. All you had to do was write on the dry surface of the mirror with a bar of soap or, if necessary, with your finger. The steam later made the message visible.

The shadowy figure did not reappear. Darren had probably just imagined it. Presumably it was only a shadow, and his tired mind along with Maggie's horror stories had turned it into a ghost.

Satisfied with that explanation, Darren grabbed the window cleaner and removed the message. Then he reattached the door handle, shut the bedroom windows, and left the former church.

He had no explanation for the relief he felt as soon as he sat in the car, but there was one thing he knew for sure: Maggie would have to pay for those pranks. With interest!

CHAPTER 9

Darren was greeted by bagpipe music when he got home. He wondered about fleeing to the pub, but when he entered the house, his grandmother immediately put the instrument away.

"How was your day, Granny?" he asked, slumping on the sofa.

"Busy. It's amazing how many visitors you get when they know you can't run away. If the plaster cast hadn't made it too difficult, I'd have escaped through the back door into the heather."

Darren grinned. "That bad?"

"Well, not really, but I do miss my walks. How is an old lady supposed to stay fit if all she does is sit at home with tea and biscuits?"

"Who came to see you?"

"In the morning, Andrew dropped in for tea and a chat. He offered to bring my shopping from Oban if I ever needed it."

"Andrew?"

"Andrew Birtwistle. The postman."

"The village casanova?"

Granny Erica's eyes widened. Then she chuckled. "Who said that?"

Darren shrugged. "Uncle Greg. Is it true?"

"Of course not! Although he's certainly something of a ladies' man. I heard he's been visiting Allison rather a lot since her husband died. And Norma often mentions that he'd popped round for a coffee or a muffin."

Darren raised an eyebrow. "Your friend Norma? Really?"

Granny Erica waved dismissively. "You know what she's like. As soon as anyone has anything interesting, she gets it too. Even if it's the flu."

"You mean the postie is something like that? Something interesting I mean, not the flu. Although, if you believe Uncle Greg, the flu might be quite fitting."

Granny Erica laughed. "Apparently so. But with me it's completely different," she hastened to add. "Andrew and I are just friends. He's interested in traditional bagpipe music, you know."

"If you say so." Darren tried not to smirk. He wasn't quite sure, but he thought his grandmother was blushing.

"Anyway, as soon as he was gone, Greg knocked on the door. It was almost like he'd been waiting outside until Andrew continued his tour."

Darren thought that quite likely. Uncle Greg had made no secret of his dislike for the postman. "How's he doing?"

"Quite well, I think. Even though he's always complaining about getting old. He stayed quite long. Only when I told him that I was expecting Norma and Janet for a cuppa, he suddenly remembered that he still had some errand to run."

"I can imagine." Darren grinned.

Granny Erica's friends both lived alone. One was widowed, the other divorced. The reason was the same for both, at least according to Greg: the women's sharp tongues had driven one husband to his grave and the other away.

It wasn't quite that bad in Darren's personal experience. Nevertheless, he preferred to be out during their visits.

"Then I had to give Janet a quick call," Granny Erica continued. "I didn't want Greg to think that I'd made up the meeting to get rid of him."

"You *did* make it up to get rid of him!" Darren pointed out.

His grandmother grinned impishly. "Anyhow, it was nice to chat with the girls, but that's why I only now got round to practising the bagpipes."

Darren nodded. "I see."

"By the way, Norma says if you have any trouble with Libby you should get in touch with her. She spanked her bahookie when she was a naughty child, and she doesn't mind doing it again."

The image of the elderly Auntie Norma putting her grown-up niece, a successful estate agent, over her knee made Darren grin. "Thanks, but tell her I'll be fine."

Granny Erica shrugged. "Suit yourself. How did your first day go?"

While they had dinner, Darren told her about his new colleague Maggie and the impressive houses they had cleaned. He ended with the former church and the pranks that Maggie had pulled on him there. He didn't mention how uncomfortable he had felt in the house when she had gone, nor that he almost believed he had seen a ghost.

After he had finished, Granny Erica looked at him thoughtfully. "Where did you say this haunted church was?"

"Over in Benderloch. Why? Will you try to convince me that it's cursed too?" Darren smiled.

"Why don't you make us another cup of tea? I need to think for a moment."

With a shrug, Darren started brewing tea for them both. When he sat down at the table again, he looked at his grandmother in anticipation, but she took her time. First, she spooned such a large amount of sugar into her tea that Darren was getting toothache just watching. Then she stirred her cup for several minutes.

Eventually Darren lost his patience. "So what are you pondering?"

"Did Maggie admit that she tricked you?"

He laughed. "Of course not. She was trying to convince me a poltergeist or some other evil presence in the house was responsible. Why do you ask?"

His grandmother hesitated. "I'm not sure, but there is this story about an old kirk in Benderloch. Maybe it's something to do with your apparition."

Darren rolled his eyes. "There was no apparition. Maggie was just taking the piss."

Granny Erica raised a conciliatory hand. "I'm not saying there was. I just want you to know the history."

"So what did happen there?" Darren was getting riled. It had been a long day, and he wasn't particularly keen on hearing another ghost story.

"Alright, listen. About a hundred years ago, there was a minister over in Benderloch. Reverend Stuart Rees, I think he was called. He was a young fellow, fresh from college."

"And he's supposed to be haunting the place?" Darren interrupted her doubtfully.

"Well, no. Or maybe. Let me tell you the story first! Anyway, he was quite a prankster. He loved practical jokes."

"A minister?"

Granny Erica shrugged. "Clerics are people too, and some even have a sense of humour."

Despite himself, Darren had to smile. He remembered the old 'Reverend Snore', whose boring sermons his mother had dragged him to every Sunday for a while after separating from his father. That one could have done with a bit of humour to liven up his lectures.

"What did the minister do?"

"Oh, all sorts. His church services were a real trial for his flock. His pranks ranged from spicy communion wafers to hymn books glued to the pews. You can imagine how difficult it must have been not to swear in church. Of course, nobody could say anything during service.

"Someone said he even messed about with some of the pews, so they'd make farting noises when anyone moved. In any case, his sense of humour wasn't appreciated. You know, back then people took their religion a lot more seriously."

"They probably considered him an accessory of the Devil," Darren grinned.

Granny Erica nodded. "Yet he was a very devout man himself. He just had a slightly different take on the Almighty. God is joy, he tried to convince his congregation. A cheerful heart is good medicine. Even the bible says so. The good people of his flock did not agree, apparently. No godliness without sacrifice and humility for them. Laughter, especially in a house of God, was deeply suspect."

"So they sent him to Hell? Or did they try an exorcist first?"

His grandmother shook her head. "Neither. He died in a tragic accident, but it was his own fault."

Darren looked at her expectantly. "You mean, he bumped himself off? Like those idiots at the Darwin Awards?"

Granny Erica looked at him in confusion. "Darwin Awards?"

He rolled his eyes. "I'll show you some time. On the internet."

"If you say so."

"So what happened?"

"The accident? That was a strange story. Nobody ever found out what Reverend Rees intended when he got himself into a situation that cost him his life. Was it meant as a morbid joke to cheer up the family of a recently deceased parishioner? Quite possibly. In any case, he took the deceased, who had already been laid out in the church, into the vestry and hid himself in the coffin in his place. There he waited. When the time came for the funeral service, the congregation gathered in respectful silence. Only Reverend Rees didn't turn up. Probably someone discreetly knocked on the door to the vestry, but nobody was there. Even though that didn't mean no body was there," Granny Erica chuckled.

"Eventually a brother of the deceased rode to Culcharan to find another cleric. Hours had passed and the new minister didn't have much time, so the service was only a prayer and a couple of hymns. Nobody looked inside the coffin or noticed anything untoward when they nailed it shut. Then they buried it."

Darren's eyes went wide. "With the minister in it? That's horrible! Wouldn't he have heard the funeral going on around him? Why didn't he jump out of the coffin then? Or at the very least he could have shouted when they nailed him in."

"Nobody knows what happened. He may have fallen asleep while waiting, or he passed out from lack of oxygen."

"And nobody noticed? Are you sure he got into the coffin by himself? It could have been some vengeful parishioners."

Granny Erica shook her head. "No, it's pretty certain it was him. As it turned out, he hadn't just hidden the deceased in the vestry. He also put a sign in his hands. 'Do not disturb! Waiting for resurrection.' Nobody but the minister would have done that. They also found the key to the vestry in his pocket later, although it took quite a while until they did.

"For days people wondered where Reverend Rees had gone, until the increasing stench from the vestry finally prompted someone to check in there. They had to break down the door, because, as I said, Reverend Rees still had the key. You can imagine the shock when they found the dead man in their kirk. When they recognised the body, they immediately wondered who they had buried instead. That's how it all came out in the end."

Darren shook his head. "A great story," he admitted. "But it doesn't mean the dead minister is now haunting his old kirk. Quite apart from me not believing in ghosts: wouldn't a switched-off mains socket and a swapped can of furniture polish be a bit lame for a prankster like Rees?"

Granny Erica shrugged. "How am I supposed to know? I just thought you should know the story. Incidentally, your grandfather sometimes talked about wanting to set the ghost of Rees free. So maybe there is something to it. Unfortunately, he never got the chance."

"Grandpa Alan believed in ghosts?"

His grandmother shook her head. "I wouldn't put it like that. He didn't just believe in them. He could see them."

"My grandad could see ghosts?" Darren repeated incredulously.

"He called them spirits. But yes. I thought you knew that. I always assumed you were interested in the paranormal because you wanted to see them too."

Darren frowned. He couldn't remember that his grandfather supposedly was able to see ghosts, but neither did he recall why he had collected books about ghosts when he was wee. He just did.

His grandmother looked at him wistfully. "Be that as it may. That was the story of Reverend Rees, as far as I can remember it. And now I'd better go to bed."

"Alright. Thank you." A mischievous grin appeared on Darren's face. "Maybe the story can help me pay Maggie back for her tricks."

A sharp look from Granny Erica warned him to curb his enthusiasm. "Remember she's your colleague. You surely don't want to risk your new job straight away?"

"Of course not, Granny." He hung his head. But still, he wouldn't let Maggie get away completely unpunished.

"At least she won't get a chance to tease you tomorrow. I called Libby to tell her you need to take me to the hairdressers. So she's given you two other houses. You're to pick up the keys and addresses from her office."

Darren stared at her in disbelief. "You called Libby?"

"Of course. We agreed you could organize your hours so you can look after me, didn't we?"

Darren nodded, stunned. He had assumed he would be allowed to choose his own hours, but obviously he was mistaken. His grandmother and Libby Whatmough appeared to get along disturbingly well. If he didn't do something about it soon, he would have two bosses ordering him around.

CHAPTER 10

After the hard work, Darren slept like a log. At least until he started dreaming.

He found himself in a black-and-white film, which reminded him of an old American comedy called "The Canterville Ghost" that he had watched at some point. However, instead of the ghost of Sir Simon, a translucent Reverend Rees was haunting the old manor house, while Darren had to play the role of Sir Simon's cowardly descendant Private Cuffy. The ghost of the minister followed him around like a balloon on a string, wailing incessantly. "You must help me. Only you can do it."

Even in his sleep the constant whining annoyed Darren. "Why are you bothering me? I don't even believe in ghosts. Piss off!"

Yet the wailing ghost followed him from the attic to the cellar, and from the dining room to the garden. Darren even tried to punch him, even though he was never violent normally. But as you would expect with a ghost, his fist found no resistance whatsoever. The only effect was Darren getting goosebumps when his arm passed through the minister's cool and half-transparent apparition.

Eventually Darren gave up trying to escape. His chest tightened from exhaustion, and his breathing grew laboured. He slumped into an armchair in the drawing room of the black-and-white castle. "Alright then," he panted. "What exactly do you want?"

The ghost of the minister pointed at the carpet, where the outline of a stain could be seen. "I need more red," he confided.

"More red? In a black-and-white film?"

"And you have to scare me." The ghost cackled then burst like a balloon.

Darren woke up. For a confused moment, he wondered what this strange dream meant. Then he realised he was still struggling to breathe. He tried to take a breath, but his mouth and nose were blocked by hair. A heavy weight on his chest made breathing even harder. He flailed his arms in panic—and was rewarded with a contented purr.

"Baudrons!"

Cursing, he catapulted the cat from his chest onto the floor. Then he fell back and gasped for air. When his breathing had got back to normal, he untangled himself from his blanket and staggered across the dark room to the sink.

Ghosts! There were no ghosts, no matter how much Maggie or his grandmother tried to convince him. Nevertheless, they started haunting his dreams, and even Baudrons threw his weight behind it!

Darren gulped down a large glass of water. When he put the glass back, he shivered. Had it been this cold here before? An icy draught was wafting around his calves, yet he was sure all the windows were shut. Better to crawl back under his blanket.

He heard a dull thump from the other side of the room. When he stared into the darkness he saw something floating towards him: a pale figure with long white hair blowing in a breeze that couldn't be there. Annoyed, Darren frowned.

"Are you kidding me?"

He must have said that out loud, because the figure flinched. A blazing light came on, making him squint. He heard a door slam shut.

Then a familiar voice said, "Heavens, Darren! Are you trying to scare me to death? What are you doing sneaking about in the dark at this time of night?"

Darren cautiously opened his eyes and stared at the 'apparition' in disbelief. "Granny?" She was wearing a white nightgown. Her hair, which she usually wore in a bun, hung loosely over her thin shoulders. Her plaster cast stuck out from under the nightgown. That must have been the thumping he had heard. She had a fluffy slipper on her other foot.

Embarrassed he had mistaken his own grandmother for a ghost, he pointed to the sink. "I was thirsty. And why are you wandering about?"

She wrinkled her nose and pointed at the back door, the handle of which she was still holding on to. "I went to the loo. Not that it's any of your business, but it's what happens to people my age. And now I'm going back to bed." Her cast thumping on the floor, she disappeared into her room.

Darren stared after her bemused, then he switched off the light and trudged back to the sofa. Unfortunately Baudrons had taken his nice warm spot.

Grumbling, Darren shoved the cat off the sofa and crawled under the covers. "I really need to find a place of my own," he thought before falling asleep.

The next day, Darren wandered around Oban while his grandmother was getting her hair done. He would have used the time to see Libby, but when he phoned, she had told him that she was busy with a client. She'd be expecting him at her office after lunch instead. So he browsed the shops and wondered whether he should get a coffee—until he had an idea. Grinning, he went to look for the right shop for his plan.

A good two hours later, after an early lunch at the harbour, Darren dropped his grandmother off at her home in Ganavan. Then he drove back into town following the narrow coastal road.

Oban's centre stretched along the seafront, but only the main street and the big supermarkets to the south of it were located down here. Many of the houses clung to the slopes of Battery Hill rising behind the main street. The hill was crowned by McCaig's Tower, a grey, ring-shaped building that looked a little like the Colosseum in Rome and offered magnificent views over the town and across to the islands.

Libby Whatmough's estate agency was in a good location on Dalriach Road. Like most streets snaking up Battery Hill it was rather narrow. But Libby's office not only had a wonderful view of the town centre and the harbour, but also boasted three dedicated parking spaces. One for her own BMW and two for her well-heeled clients.

Darren parked the red Corsa in one of the customer spaces and went to the door. The office was locked, and nobody was in sight. Apparently he was early. It was lunchtime. Libby was probably still out and her assistant, if she had one, had gone for lunch. As he couldn't start work without the keys to the houses, there was nothing to do but wait.

He passed the time by studying the property adverts in the window. The houses on offer were scattered all over Argyll, with some further afield in the Highlands. A quick glance at the prices confirmed that most of them were unaffordable. There were cheaper properties available on some of the smaller islands, but who wanted to live on a tiny piece of rock that provided few jobs and often got cut off for days on end during the winter storms?

"Have you found something suitable?"

Darren spun around in surprise. Libby stood behind him smiling archly. She was carrying a box from a nearby Indian take-away.

"I expect the wages I'm paying you won't be quite enough for that."

She pointed at the advert that was right in front of Darren. A lavishly modernised Victorian villa with eleven bedrooms and a large garden. The price tag read one point five million pounds.

Darren wryly shook his head. "Shame really. I quite fancied that one."

Before he followed Libby into the office, he took one last wistful look at the only two rental flats he had spotted among the other adverts. Unfortunately, even those were well out of his price range.

Libby was already holding a couple of keys and a piece of paper with the addresses on it. When she noticed Darren's look, she tilted her head. "Are you really looking for a place?"

Darren hesitated, then shook his head. "I'll find something."

Libby gave him a piercing glance. "Are you getting uncomfortable on your grandmother's sofa yet?"

His mouth fell open. "How did you know I'm sleeping on the sofa?"

She laughed. "What do you think? I'm in the property business. I know the old croft houses don't usually have an attic that can be converted. One room for sleeping and one for everything else. If she retained it completely original, there's an outhouse round the back. Those old stone houses look idyllic, and many tourists imagine it would be romantic to live there, but they're far too small for a family. So, assuming you don't want to sleep in your granny's bedroom, the couch is your only option." Her eyes sparkled with amusement.

Darren conceded.

"So what are you looking for? A small flat? A furnished room?"

"Actually, a room in a flat share would be enough for me. Or a studio. As long as it's cheap. But I don't expect you've got anything like that."

He looked around her office. The desk was white with steel legs. Understated, but certainly expensive. There were also a small coffee table and two armchairs. White of course. The espresso machine on the sideboard looked big enough for a coffee bar. The whole office smelled of money. Lots of money.

When he turned back towards Libby, she seemed to ponder something. "I suppose I could find you something, but you'd have to get these two houses shipshape today.

With this one," she pointed at the second address, "the owner has passed away, so it's a bit dusty and overgrown. But I have a viewing there tomorrow, and I'd prefer not to be embarrassed."

Darren grinned. "Of course. If you can find me a cheap room, I'll do anything."

He grabbed the two keys and the addresses. Libby meanwhile sat down at her desk and started poking around in her lunch box with a fork.

"How did it go yesterday?" she asked casually.

Darren froze. Had Maggie said anything to their boss? "Fine?"

Libby looked up from her lunch. "Is that a question?"

"No. I mean, it went well. Maggie and I got along great. She's a real professional."

The estate agent scrutinised his face carefully. "But?"

"No but. It was fun."

He had clearly laid it on too thick. Libby slowly put her fork down. "Do tell. What's wrong?"

"Nothing."

Libby's eyes narrowed.

"Nothing important," Darren quickly amended. "Nothing that affects work in any case. Maggie just tried to convince me that the old kirk in Benderloch is haunted."

Libby sighed.

Darren hastened to add, "But that's all nonsense, of course. She was just winding up the new guy. After all, ghosts don't exist. So it's nothing to get riled up about."

Libby sighed again and picked up her fork. "I hoped she'd pull herself together with you. Maggie is great, no doubt about that, but unfortunately she's quite superstitious."

"Really? I don't think it's that bad. I'm sure she was just teasing me." Darren was annoyed with himself. Of course he wanted to get back at Maggie for her pranks, but he hadn't intended to rat on her to their boss.

Libby looked at him doubtfully. "Let's hope you're right, but make sure she doesn't repeat her ghost stories to customers. If it affects her work, let me know."

Darren nodded. He certainly would not do that. While Libby took a bite of her now cold curry, he waved the bunch of keys at her.

"I better get going," he called. He left before Libby could ask any more questions about the previous day.

CHAPTER 11

The first address turned out to be a holiday home. According to Libby he was only supposed to sort out its small garden as it was currently occupied. But he hadn't even got the lawnmower out of the shed when the lady renting the house cornered him.

She asked whether he was from the estate agency.

"Yes."

Did he know that the window in the bedroom didn't close properly?

"No, but I'm not—"

"The shower is dripping constantly, and the boiler is very unreliable."

Darren tried to point out that he was only there to do the gardening and that she should take up her concerns with Ms Whatmough, who would send a plumber round if necessary. But the woman wasn't deterred and kept on complaining. Eventually he turned his back and began unwinding the cable of the electric lawnmower. Meanwhile she continued talking to his back unabated. When he tried to get past her to get to the garden, she blocked his way holding out her arms. Her face had turned an unhealthy shade of purple.

Darren stopped. A few seconds more, and she'll have a stroke, he thought. Although that seemed quite an attractive prospect to get her to shut up at last, it would probably cause new trouble. The lawn mowing would have to wait until an ambulance arrived to take her away.

Also, Libby probably wouldn't be too impressed if her guest collapsed right in front of one of her employees.

In the end, Darren relented and followed the woman around the house to record the alleged defects. Or at least he pretended to. During the hour it took her and the increasingly impatient Darren to look at everything and document it on his phone, her colour improved from purple to a rich tomato red.

When he had finished, the woman looked at him, shrewd and calculating.

Given all these problems, nobody could expect her husband to pay the full rent, she declared. Surely this shabby hovel wasn't worth more than half that.

Darren cursed inwardly for allowing himself to be used like that. He should have seen this coming, he thought.

"I'm really sorry, but I'm definitely not authorised to negotiate the price with you. I will of course inform Ms Whatmough," he promised.

She smiled like a hungry shark.

Stupid cow! Back in Edinburgh, he would have made it quite clear what he thought of her. But he knew where that would lead, and he couldn't afford to lose his job just now. Libby wouldn't be happy with him as it was. He doubted that she would help him find a room after this performance.

Finally, the woman graciously allowed him to attend to his actual tasks. At least she didn't follow him and the lawnmower around to point out every overlooked blade of grass, as Darren had almost expected.

Before he drove to the other property, Darren rang Libby. She laughed when he told her how her guest had dragged him around the house insisting that he recorded every little defect.

"Those two do that every year, and every year they end up paying the agreed price. They're renting the house at pre-season prices, yet they still try for another discount. I should have warned you, but I didn't think they'd start on you straight away."

"No problem," Darren said. "Next time I'll just wait until she drops dead." Inwardly, he kicked himself. Why hadn't he thought of phoning Libby straight away?

"You didn't only just leave the house, did you? I told you how important it is to get Rose Cottage into perfect shape."

"Of course not," Darren lied. "I'm just taking a short break."

"And? How are you getting on?"

"All fine. I'm nearly finished."

"Really?" Libby sounded surprised.

Darren hastily rowed back. "There are a few more odds and ends to do, but nothing you need to worry about. By the way, when exactly is the viewing?"

"That's all right then. The appointment is at half past ten, but I'll be there at ten. Just in case you've missed anything."

"I'm sure I won't. Don't worry."

He hung up. Now he could only hope that the house was in a better state than Libby's tone suggested.

Rose Cottage looked completely different to what Darren had expected. It was neither a cottage, nor was it particularly old. Instead, it was one of about a half dozen identical bungalows in Pennyfuir, a tiny hamlet east of Ganavan.

Its only notable feature was its bright blue coat of paint. It was surrounded by a small garden full of overgrown rose bushes as well as some other shrubs Darren didn't recognise. The untended lawn was still greyish brown from the winter. A huge tree towered over the house and part of the neighbouring garden. A place like Sleeping Beauty's castle, an estate agent might have claimed, but to Darren it looked more like a thorny jungle.

He groaned. If the house was as bad inside as it looked from the outside, Libby better forgot about her viewing appointment. He parked in front of the garage and looked for the right key to open the front door.

The air inside smelled stale, as if nobody had opened a window for weeks or even months. The house was furnished, but not like a holiday home. Most pieces dated back at least forty years. Still, the last owner of the house had clearly been proud of it. The furniture may have been old, but it was in immaculate condition. A bit of an airing, some ABBA hits on the record player, and you could feel like you had time-travelled back to the Seventies—the era of flared trousers and garishly coloured fashion.

Darren grinned and opened the windows in all the rooms. Then he grabbed a duster and some furniture polish, which he found in a cupboard under the sink, and started working.

He knew there wouldn't be time to clean the whole house and then sort out the garden afterwards, but Maggie was right, the most important thing was to suggest cleanliness. Nobody was going to move in straight away, and the scent of furniture polish would go a long way. Maybe he could persuade Libby to invest in a selection of potpourri or scented candles.

Luckily, the floor looked acceptable. But the brown pattern of the carpet wouldn't show much dirt anyway. Instead, he wiped the chrome fittings in the bathroom and kitchen. Once those were nice and shiny, they would hopefully distract from anything he might have missed.

When Darren was satisfied with the interior, he put the cleaning stuff away and went outside for a closer look at the overgrown garden. By now the sun was starting to set, so he would have to be quick if he wanted to see what he was doing.

The first thing he needed was a hedge trimmer, preferably a strong petrol-powered one that would make short work of those rose bushes. But all he found in the garage were some manual clippers that were little more than an oversized pair of scissors. After some more searching he discovered a chainsaw. Maybe he could use that? On closer inspection, he realised that the chain was broken. No luck again. At least the lawnmower seemed okay. It was old, petrol-driven and—as he soon discovered—bone dry.

Darren cursed. He stuck his head out of the garage and surveyed the thorny jungle in the front garden, which was slowly disappearing in the dusk. What was the point of a house smelling of furniture polish if Libby and the potential buyers needed a machete to cross the garden? He sighed.

Maybe he should just call it a day. Libby could have warned him what state the house was in, instead of sending him to the whingers in the holiday cottage first. Or she could have postponed the viewing for a couple of days. It was her own fault!

He slammed the garage door shut and sat in his car. He could almost see it: Libby arriving at the house half an hour early. How she would fume when she saw the overgrown garden. Would she attempt to save the day? He tried to imagine her wielding the clippers wearing high heels and an expensive skirt suit. No, that was definitely not going to happen. Instead, she would tell her aunt and his grandmother, who would be very disappointed in him.

Darren cursed again. He didn't care much about what Aunt Norma would think, but his grandmother had always stood by him. Even when he had told his mother that he wasn't interested in business studies. And Libby would never help him find somewhere to live if he left her hanging.

He stomped back into the garage, grabbed the lawnmower's petrol canister and threw it into the boot of the car. Then he took the clippers. If he went to get petrol now, it would be pitch black by the time he got back. So he needed to do the lawn first thing tomorrow. But he could still cut back the rose bushes lining the path, so that Libby and her customers could at least get through to the front door without getting trapped in the thorns.

Three, four, five tendrils fell. When he bent down to move them aside, the thorns pricked his hand. Damn roses! No wonder Sleeping Beauty had to nap for a hundred years before someone was stupid enough to take them on. Bloody finger in mouth, he stomped back to the garage. It was dark in there, even with the faint light of the single lightbulb that came on after he had flicked the switch. After some searching, he found a pair of old work gloves and a bag for garden waste.

Meanwhile, the sun had set, leaving behind a deep blue sky. The garden was sinking into darkness.

Darren grumpily stuffed unruly rose cuttings into the bag. While the gloves protected his hands, the thorns still scratched his arms. When he finally got the bushes under some control, he realised that the roses had ripped a hole in his sweatshirt. He cursed. Why couldn't there be just grass in the front garden? He wouldn't mind a few daisies. Even garden gnomes, which were ugly, but easy to tend to. Yet instead someone planted this godawful thorny mess. He angrily attacked the roses with the clippers.

"Sue won't like that at all," someone said.

"Eh?" Darren looked around.

An old man had appeared between the rose bushes, just a few steps away. He must have sneaked in from next door somehow, because if he had come from the street, he would have had to pass Darren. The old man stood in the shade of the house. He had snow-white hair, an athletic build like a farmer or fisherman and was a bit taller than average. As far as Darren could make out in the dark, he was wearing dungarees, wellies and a sun hat, strangely enough. When he saw that Darren had noticed him, the old man shook his head and looked accusingly at the tattered roses and the cuttings that covered the garden path.

"No," he declared. "Sue certainly won't like this. She's so proud of her roses."

Darren looked at the carnage he had caused. While the path was now free, at least once he had picked up the cuttings, the rose bushes did look rather ragged. So what? Libby surely would be more concerned that prospective buyers didn't tear their clothes.

"I'm sure they'll grow back in no time," Darren decided.

He turned around and continued snipping bits off the roses. With that meddlesome neighbour watching him, he worked a bit more slowly and carefully.

"Still, you shouldn't be treating Sue's roses like that," he heard the old man saying reproachfully.

"If she doesn't like it, she should have cut them herself," Darren replied without turning around. Why didn't this funny old geezer leave him alone?

"But she's in the hospital!"

Darren lowered the clippers and turned towards the man. "I'm sorry to hear that. It can't be nice to be in hospital while it's spring outside."

The man nodded wistfully. "I wish I could help her. She's been away for an awfully long time. But I don't even manage to look after the house, let alone her garden."

Darren didn't say anything.

"But you've been in the house, haven't you? Did social services send you? Are you tidying up because Sue will come home soon?" The old man's voice sounded hopeful.

"Home? What do you mean?"

"That Sue will come home to her house, of course."

An unpleasant thought occurred to Darren. Was it possible that the old man didn't know his neighbour had died? He cleared his throat. "Was it long ago that she had to go to hospital?"

The man wrung his hands nervously. "To be honest, I don't know. Since I'm dead, I really struggle to keep track of time. But it must have been quite some time ago."

Darren blinked. Had he heard right? 'Since I'm dead?' The old man probably meant since he retired. That he hadn't heard from her for a long time confirmed Darren's suspicion. He sighed. "I'm very sorry. But do you think Sue might have died in hospital?"

The old man shook his head vigorously. "Impossible. She would have told me."

"She would have told you that she died?"

"But of course! Besides, she's always been in very good health. Why would she suddenly die? What made you even say something like that?" The old man's eyes flashed angrily and he clenched his fists.

Darren took a step back and raised his hands in apology. "I'm really sorry about your neighbour, but I'm here on behalf of an estate agent called Libby Whatmough. I'm fairly certain she said that the owner of the house had died. Besides, there are no personal belongings left in the house. Just the furniture."

"Just the furniture? That can't be right! What is she supposed to wear when she comes back?" The old man fidgeted nervously. There were tears in his eyes now.

Darren was uncomfortable with the old man's feelings. He turned around and looked across the garden. "I'm so sorry," he mumbled.

When he turned back moments later, the old man had vanished. "What the...?" Darren blinked in confusion. Where had he gone? Was there a shortcut to the neighbouring property? He couldn't see one. And how could the old codger sneak away so quietly in his wellies? At his age too!

After a moment, Darren shrugged his shoulders and decided that he didn't care. Glad that the weird old man was gone, he turned his attention back to the roses. Even though it wasn't any of that coffin dodger's business, he now treated the plants much more carefully. Out of respect for the late Sue.

When Libby arrived at Rose Cottage the next morning, Darren had just finished cleaning the windows in the living room. He had been working since eight o'clock.

He had mown the lawn and tidied up some of the worst damage to the rose bushes. In the light of the morning sun, he had also noticed that the windows were rather dirty, so he had grumpily cleaned those as well. The strange neighbour had not turned up again.

Libby was impressed. "I didn't think you'd get the house into such a good state. Especially considering you only started at four yesterday."

Darren looked at her in surprise. "How did you know that?"

Libby laughed. "Did you really expect me to believe that you only called about the holiday cottage once you'd finished here? To be honest, I was fully expecting to have to cancel on the Thomases."

The humming of a car engine made them look up. Shortly after, a red post van parked on the other side of the road. The postman waved at them. When he recognised Libby, he sauntered over.

"Hello Ms Whatmough. Trying to extend my route again?" he asked with a smile. Then he looked at Darren, frowning as he tried to place him.

"This is Darren Bagshaw," Libby introduced him. "Andrew Birtwistle."

Darren nodded and eyed the postman curiously. So this was the guy Uncle Greg disliked so much. The village casanova. Darren could immediately understand why Greg was suspicious. For a guy who must be in his fifties at least, he was rather good-looking. His short hair was mottled grey, his face tanned and striking. The sight of him probably reminded many an old lady of a younger George Clooney, Darren thought with amusement.

Libby seemed to know Birtwistle pretty well too, although Darren didn't get the impression that she was particularly happy to see him.

The postman had been scrutinising Darren. Suddenly he slapped his forehead. "Bagshaw! I should have guessed straight away. You must be Erica's grandson. You have your grandmother's eyes." He beamed.

"Certainly not." Darren replied drily. "She needs them herself."

Birtwistle laughed. "I suppose that's true!" But he seemed glad to turn his attention back to Libby. "So you'll be showing someone round Mrs Shepherd's old place today?"

Libby nodded. "Yep."

"Do you think they will buy it? It's not a bad house, is it?"

She smiled indulgently. "If I could tell you beforehand, selling houses would be so easy, anyone could do it. Even you."

The postman smiled too, apparently not in the least offended. "I'm sure you're right. So I guess we'll just have to wait and see who our new neighbours will be. Good luck anyway!"

"Thank you."

When nobody said anything else, the postman started drumming his fingers on his postbag. "Well, I guess I'd better be on my way."

Libby nodded. Birtwistle hesitated briefly before he turned to start his round of the neighbouring houses.

"Rather nosy," Darren commented.

His boss sighed and shook her head in resignation. "You can say that again."

"What happened to the former owners of this house?" Darren suddenly asked.

"You mean the Shepherds? There was only an elderly widow. When she died, her nephew inherited her home. But he wasn't interested and asked me to sell it."

"Was her name Sue?"

Libby thought about it. "Susan, I think. Why do you ask?"

Darren told her about the strange old man who had appeared in the garden yesterday, and who hadn't yet heard about the widow's death.

"An old man?" Libby frowned. "Are you sure he wasn't some homeless guy?"

"Pretty sure. He seemed to know this Susan quite well. Maybe he's a neighbour."

Libby considered that while looking at the other houses in the hamlet. Then she shook her head. "If he lived here, he'd have noticed the removal van. The nephew was here once or twice as well. In any case, I can't think of anyone living here who'd fit your description. There's a married couple living next door, and a family with children next to them. To be honest, I don't know of any single old man living up here. He just walked into the garden last night?"

Darren nodded.

The estate agent wrinkled her nose. "Don't mention that to any of my customers, please. I don't want them to think there's some creepy stalker hanging around. Understood? Maybe you should ask the neighbours though. Perhaps someone knows him. And if not, they might want to keep their eyes open. In their own best interest."

Darren thought that was a bit of an overreaction. The old man had seemed harmless enough. Maybe he had simply wandered up from a retirement home nearby. Nevertheless, Darren was curious to hear what the neighbours would say about him.

CHAPTER 12

Darren and Maggie spent the afternoon cleaning another of the estate agent's houses. Neither of them mentioned what had happened in the 'haunted house' two days before. Instead, they chatted about the beautiful Georgian building they were working in and gossiped about Libby's well-heeled clientele.

He marvelled that she had so many picturesque old croft houses and historic manor houses in her portfolio. "Looking at the adverts in the window of her office, you'd think Argyll was just one big film set, when there's plenty of run-down and ugly places as well. Why doesn't Libby sell anything affordable?"

Maggie shrugged her shoulders. "She just doesn't need to. Sometimes I think she's getting more work than she can handle, especially when it comes to inheritances. An old auntie or doddering grandad kicks the bucket, and soon the heirs run down her door because they want to cash in on the family home."

"How do the greedy relatives know her? If they don't want the houses themselves, I suppose they live in London or overseas or wherever. How do they know which agent to approach in Oban? There must be plenty of them. Does Libby attend the funerals to catch them there? Or does she put adverts in the obituary section of the Oban Times?"

"No idea. Maybe she gets funeral parlours to print her contact details on the bills for coffins." Maggie grinned.

"She could certainly run her own antique shop, what with the number of old shacks we have to clear out every year."

Maggie clearly was in a good mood and even volunteered to polish the parquet flooring on the ground floor of the villa, a strenuous job that would probably have been Darren's otherwise. Instead, she sent him to fetch coffee and muffins for their afternoon break.

Darren suspected it was a peace offering, but he wasn't going to forgive her the pranks in the haunted house that easily. All the better if she felt safe for now. There would be an opportunity to pay her back properly at some point.

Libby called shortly before it was time to finish for the day. Apparently her customers had forgotten a scarf in Rose Cottage.

"Could you drop by quickly and bring it to my office? As you're taking tomorrow off, you surely don't mind doing me a wee favour."

That caught Darren off guard. "I'm taking tomorrow off?"

"Of course. Your grandmother called me half an hour ago."

"I see," Darren grumbled.

He pulled a face, causing Maggie to give him a questioning look. He rolled his eyes and pointed at his phone.

This definitely had to stop! It was outrageous that Libby knew first when he had to do something for his grandmother. And that Granny Erica was talking to his boss behind his back.

"So will you do it?" Libby's impatient question snapped him out of his thoughts.

"Sure. No problem."

"Thanks! See you later then."

Maggie only shrugged when Darren explained Libby's sudden request. He left the rest of the work to her and made his way to Rose Cottage.

At least he would be able to use the opportunity to ask the neighbours about the old man. By now most of them should be back from work, and Libby surely wouldn't mind.

He parked his grandmother's red Corsa in front of the empty house and decided to head over to the neighbours' first. He tried to make his way through the bushes just like the old man must have done the night before. But after a few steps he found his way blocked by a fence. A perfectly manicured lawn stretched from there to the neighbouring house. The old codger couldn't have come this way then.

Darren went back to the street to get round to the neighbours' front door. The garden of their house not only had a carefully trimmed lawn, but also two neatly laid out flower beds with three rows of spring flowers in each. What a contrast to the garden of Rose Cottage, whose sprawling shrubbery still was a tangled mess, despite Darren's efforts with the clippers and lawnmower.

'Mr & Mrs Stickle' it said on the door. The doorbell was answered by a woman who was probably in her forties, who eyed him with undisguised suspicion.

"Yes?"

Darren explained who he was and what he wanted.

Instead of replying, she cast an appraising glance towards the neighbouring property. The rear of his car was visible behind a sprawling bush.

"You were here yesterday, and this morning as well," she observed.

Darren nodded. "Ms Whatmough had a viewing appointment for the house today. I work for her."

"Well, I hope the people she brought were decent. We don't want to get hippies like the Shepherds as neighbours again."

Darren had to suppress a grin. He didn't know anything about the Shepherds, but he found it difficult to imagine a rose-tending little lady in her seventies as a weed-smoking hippie. On the other hand, her garden was so overgrown that it could easily be hiding some special plants. Besides, who could say what had happened in a remote village like this back in the Sixties. Maybe Mrs Shepherd really had been a hippie back then.

As he looked at Mrs Stickle with her rust-coloured hair and her old-fashioned tweed skirt, he discarded that thought. Presumably anyone who didn't cut their lawn twice a week was a hippie to her. Time to bring their conversation back to his intended topic.

"Have you seen an old man walking about next door recently? He was wearing wellies and dungarees."

Mrs Stickle's eyes narrowed, and she pouted while she thought about the question. Then she shook her head. "No."

"Do you know whether Mrs Shepherd was friends with an elderly gentleman who visited her regularly?" After all, the old man did seem to know Sue Shepherd pretty well.

Maybe he used to visit more often and just hadn't been here for a while.

Mrs Stickle shook her head. "She never had any visitors, apart from the postman, who sometimes stayed a while. Although she certainly didn't get that many letters. Not enough for him to drink tea at hers so often. A real slacker, that's what our dear postie is." She nodded in self-righteous indignation.

"Nobody else visited her then?"

She sighed theatrically and contorted her face into a sad expression, which might have been intended to show pity, if Darren hadn't seen the mean-spirited glint in her eyes. "Marcy from the Women's Institute visited occasionally. She helped her a bit around the house, even though the old bird was in surprisingly good shape still."

Darren wondered if she was just envious of the free help Sue had got.

"She lived all alone, of course," the neighbour continued. "Anthony, her husband, died years ago, and her only nephew lives somewhere down south. Near Newcastle, or so I heard. He hardly ever visited her. I was surprised she hadn't sold her house long ago and moved into an old folks' home. Such an old dear and always on her own." She sighed again, but Darren didn't buy her pretend sympathy. "You can see for yourself what has become of her garden. Not that it used to be much better when she was still around. The rabbits are her fault, too. They live the good life in that jungle, then come over to dig up our lovely lawn."

She sniffed. By now she must have forgotten that she was supposed to play the compassionate neighbour, because she went on, "Hopefully things will be better with the new neighbours. They could chop down that monster of a tree as well. You wouldn't believe the leaves we get on our lawn every autumn. And whenever there's a storm, I die a thousand deaths worrying about it falling on our home."

She gave the tree a venomous look, even though it was early spring and it didn't have any leaves yet. Darren reckoned the tree could only land on the Stickles' house if a hurricane picked it up and carried it through the air, but he nodded sympathetically anyway.

"Thank you very much for taking the time to talk to me, Mrs Stickle. Maybe you could also ask Mr Stickle whether he noticed anything or anyone." Darren didn't hold his breath though, as she was clearly the nosy type who don't miss anything happening in their neighbourhood. Her husband could hardly know more.

Mrs Stickle nodded, then cast a last venomous look at the neighbouring garden with its overgrown shrubs. She was about to close the door, but then she paused.

"I thought of something else, although I probably shouldn't say anything. I wouldn't want you to think I'm some kind of gossip who is always spying on her neighbours."

Darren raised his hand in protest and looked her straight in the eye. "I would never think something like that, Mrs Stickle!"

She seemed satisfied. Her eyes sparkled when she leaned close enough for a confidential whisper. "Actually there was an old bloke who visited her every now and then. I don't know about him wearing wellies, but he always wore a chequered shirt. A rather tall man. Quite sprightly and tanned and with a neatly trimmed white beard. For somebody of his age he was still handsome. I think he came from Ganavan. We had a quick chat once. His name was Wigeon or something like that. He said he used to work with her husband. It's none of my business, of course. But I don't think I'd be visiting the widow of a former colleague every week if I was in his shoes." She shook her head in disapproval. "Well, maybe he hoped old Sue would leave him something in her will. Although he wasn't that young himself, of course. In any case, he drove a blue Ford. A Ford Focus, I think."

"Thank you," Darren said. He had a hunch who the old man might be. Even though he didn't want to provide the nosy neighbour with any more gossip, he was curious whether he was right. "Could the name of the man have been Gudgeon?"

Mrs Stickle nodded vigorously. "That's it. Gudgeon. His first name was something old-fashioned. Gregory or Graham or some such. Do you think he's the man you're looking for?"

Darren shook his head. "I don't think so, but thank you very much." Uncle Greg and Mrs Shepherd? If that was true, he definitely wanted to know more about it.

Mrs Stickle seemed disappointed. "You're welcome. I'll keep an eye out in any case. If you could just let me know when the Shepherds' house is sold?"

Darren mumbled something non-committal and said goodbye. Mrs Stickle gave him one last, somewhat regretful look and closed the door.

At the next house, Darren struggled to get a word in about the old man. The family's three children were on their way to swimming lessons at the leisure centre in Oban. Judging by their mother's stress levels, they were running late.

"Sorry, what did you want again?" she asked after she had finally got her offspring into the car.

"I just wanted to ask whether you know an old gentleman who sometimes hangs around the garden of Rose Cottage?"

She frowned as she thought about the question. "Not that I know of. Susan had been living there on her own for so long. She must have been lonely, and I wish I'd been able to make more time for her." She glanced apologetically towards the children. Her eldest was just starting a fight in the back seat of the car.

"Francis Anthony!" his mother shouted, wagging a finger threateningly at him. Then she turned back to Darren. "I'm sorry, but we really have to get going."

He nodded in understanding.

After quickly checking on her children, she got into the car and sped off.

Darren went to see the third and final neighbour. He rang the doorbell several times, but there was no movement in the house. Eventually he gave up and went back to Rose Cottage.

He fished the key out of his pocket and opened the front door. The sun had just set, and the house was in twilight. As he already knew the room layout, Darren didn't bother switching on the light in the hallway. He wasn't keen on being watched by Mrs Stickle. He flicked on the ceiling light in the kitchen though, and quickly found the forgotten scarf on the kitchen table. Just as he was about to leave, he heard a voice behind him.

"Is she really dead?"

Darren wheeled around. At the end of the hallway, right in front of the bedroom door, was the old man again. Just like last time, he was wearing wellies, dungarees and a sun hat.

"How did you get in here?" Darren demanded.

Darren saw the twinkle in his eyes disappear for a moment, when the old man blinked in confusion. "What do you mean? I live here."

"You live here? In this house?" Darren stared at him in disbelief. Was the guy mad?

"I've lived here for thirty-five years. Together with my wife Susan." He hesitated. "Well, apparently not anymore."

"How come that nobody knows about you? Everyone says Susan Shepherd was a widow who lived on her own."

The old man smiled. "Oh, that. That's probably because I'm dead."

Darren stared at him. "You're what?"

"I'm dead. Well, I'm a ghost."

Darren's gaze wandered from the old man's face down to his wellies. He frowned. "Are you sure? You look lively enough to me. What did you say your name was?"

"Anthony Shepherd. My wife always called me Tony. And I only look so real because I'm standing in the dark. See?"

He took a step forward and put his arm into the band of light coming from the kitchen. His hand disappeared.

Darren jumped in surprise. "Wow! That's rather a neat trick."

Tony beamed.

After watching the one-armed 'ghost' for a moment, Darren turned around. He started scanning the ceiling with his eyes.

The old man stepped back into the shadows. "What are you looking for?"

Darren briefly glanced at Tony, who was watching him curiously. Then he looked back at the ceiling and walls. When he couldn't see anything obvious, he started feeling around the top of the door frame with his fingers. Again without success. As the old man was still watching him with interest, he explained, "I'm looking for the projector."

Tony frowned. "What projector?"

"The one that generates your image. Who put you up to this? Was it Maggie? Is she there with you somewhere and laughing her pretty head off?—Forget it, Maggie! I won't fall for such a cheap trick! I know there are no ghosts!"

Tony shook his head. "It's not a trick. I'm really here. Look."

He strode towards Darren. As he passed the kitchen door, he disappeared briefly and then reappeared right in front of him. He now looked a bit paler and somewhat translucent, so that Darren could see the wall behind him. Nevertheless, he was still clearly recognisable as an old man in wellies and dungarees.

Darren stared at him. He really looked impressive. Three-dimensional and rich in detail. Even his former boss wouldn't be able to afford a projector that could do that, Darren thought. Now that Tony was standing right in front of him, he could even make out some white stubble on the translucent chin of the projection. He stretched out a hand towards Tony's chest. He felt nothing at all when he touched his shirt and his fingers disappeared inside the old man's belly. Fascinated, he realised he could see his hand inside the figure. It was incredible. He just couldn't work out where or how the image was being generated.

"Stop it, that tickles!" Tony looked at him reproachfully.

He immediately pulled his hand back. "Sorry," he said automatically.

Darren and the ghost looked at each other in silence for a while. "Do you believe me now?" Tony asked eventually.

Darren hesitated. "I have to admit it's pretty clever for a projection."

Tony sighed. "What else can I do to convince you that I'm real?"

Darren reached out and flicked the light switch for the hall. The ceiling lamp cast a yellowish light on his surroundings. The apparition had disappeared. When he switched the light off again, Tony was back. The old man frowned at him.

"Are you quite finished?"

Darren shrugged. A projector might be outshone by an additional light source, so his experiment hadn't actually revealed anything. "Why do you care whether I believe you?"

"Because I'd like you to do something for me, and I can't talk to anyone else."

"Why not? You could talk to Libby, I mean, Ms Whatmough."

Tony stared at him. "Didn't you listen to me? She wouldn't be able to see or hear me. I'm a ghost."

"But I can see you."

"Apparently so."

"Why me of all people?"

Tony shook his head. "I don't know. Maybe you're crazy?" He grinned wryly.

Darren threw him a poisonous look. "All right, then. So, what's it like on the other side?"

"That's your question to find out whether I really am a ghost?"

Darren nodded.

The old man eyed him sceptically. "Do you know what it's like on the other side? How do you know I won't just make something up?"

Darren hesitated. "I'll give it a go."

Tony sighed. "To be honest, I can't tell you much about the afterlife. I only know what it's like to be a ghost here in our home. I wanted to wait for Sue and then go over to the other side with her, but it seems I missed my opportunity." He slumped down sadly.

"Could Sue, I mean Mrs Shepherd, could she see you?"

Tony lifted his head. "Aye, she could, but she was the only one. Until you turned up here anyway."

"So you're claiming I'm the only one who can see you now?"

"Yes, as far as I know. Apart from the neighbours' cat. Unfortunately, seeing ghosts doesn't seem to be a common skill anymore."

"But I'm sure I cannot see ghosts. I don't even believe they exist!"

"That's rather strange then. Are you absolutely certain that you can't see ghosts? You can see me, after all, and I'm sure I'm a ghost."

Darren shook his head and turned to leave. This weird conversation was going in circles. He was obviously overworked and starting to hallucinate.

"Wait!" Tony silently rushed past him, or through him to be more precise, and stood in front of the door. "I wanted to ask you a favour."

Darren groaned. "What do you need?" No harm in asking. It didn't mean Darren would actually have to do what his hallucination wanted.

"It's about my wife Susan. You said she died in hospital? Could you find out what she died of?"

Darren frowned. "I don't see how."

"But she's always been healthy. Strong as an ox. I can't believe she just died like that." Tony looked at him pleadingly.

Darren shrugged his shoulders. "Old people die. Maybe she was sad because she'd been alone for so long."

Tony scowled. "But she wasn't alone! She had me!"

Darren contemplated that. "If I promise to ask around a bit, will you let me go?"

Tony floated aside. "Of course!"

"But I'm not saying I'll be able to find out anything," Darren clarified.

Then he opened the door and hurried out. He jumped into his car and made a quick getaway.

Darren hadn't quite reached the end of the street when something occurred to him. He put the car in reverse and sped along the road until he was back in front of Rose Cottage.

Without paying any attention to the ghost still floating about, Darren rushed into the kitchen and grabbed the scarf. This time he remembered to switch off the light. Then he slammed the front door shut behind him and locked it.

He had definitely had enough of Rose Cottage and its strange ghost for the day.

CHAPTER 13

On the way home, Darren decided not to tell his grandmother about his encounter with the late Anthony Shepherd. At best, she would think he was overworked and going a bit crazy. At worst, she would start talking about Grandpa Alan and his gift again, and he really didn't have any patience left for that today.

First, he wanted to think it through in peace and quiet. There had to be a logical explanation for what had happened. It was impossible that he had seen an actual ghost. The apparition had looked convincing, and he hadn't been able to find a projector or microphones, but ghosts simply did not exist. He had read enough about paranormal phenomena to know all the tricks and self-deception that usually lay behind them, and he was quite certain he would eventually find out how and—more importantly—by whom he was being tricked.

He wished he had the books by Randi and Radford to hand, which described in detail how such scams were carried out. But they were back in his room in Edinburgh along with the rest of his belongings. Darren groaned. He had almost forgotten about that. Presumably his pal Tarus had chucked his stuff into boxes by now to hide them from his girlfriend. Yet another thing that he still needed to sort out.

The next morning, Darren was no closer to an explanation for what he had seen. He had spent hours mulling over how the illusion could have been created, and even longer wondering why. He had made fun of Maggie, but their little difference in opinion didn't justify that much effort or expense, did it? Besides, when would she have had time to set it all up? In the end, he had fallen asleep without coming to any conclusions.

Darren resolved to go back to the house later that day. He would find out what was going on. He was sure of that.

For now, there was something else he had to do, because Libby had been right. Darren didn't have time to work for her today. Instead, he had to take his grandmother to the hospital in Oban for an X-ray.

"It's completely unnecessary, of course," Granny Erica explained. "It's just that Doctor Nugent feels better if he gets another look at my foot."

"Uh-huh," Darren muttered as he drove his grandmother's car along the coastal road to Oban.

If it was up to her, the cast would probably come off today and by tomorrow she would be hurtling around in her little red speedster herself again.

They parked outside the hospital and Darren helped his grandmother to the entrance.

"Leave me, I'll be fine," she claimed before they even stepped through the door. "I'm not that old and frail yet."

Darren carefully let go of her so she could hobble to reception by herself.

"I'll just wait here then," he called after her. She waved her hand impatiently, which he interpreted as agreement.

He wondered whether Doctor Nugent was the reason she felt she had to walk by herself. Was she trying to impress him? A grown-up grandson accompanying her certainly wouldn't help with that. Darren smiled to himself while watching her go.

Five minutes later he entered the hospital himself. Not because he was feeling unwell, but because he was getting bored with waiting outside. At least he could find himself a coffee, even if he didn't have high hopes for the hospital cafeteria.

The young nurse who was on duty at reception watched him expectantly. Before he could approach though, an elderly lady, presumably a patient, appeared from one of the side wings. She seemed upset as she gesticulated and muttered to herself before quickly stepping up to reception and cutting Darren off.

The nurse gave him an apologetic look before she turned to the patient. Darren looked around the entrance hall. The arrow pointing towards the cafeteria was not difficult to spot. Meanwhile, the patient was still talking at the nurse. As he walked past, he winked at her and was rewarded with a smile.

The cafeteria was fairly quiet. Sitting at one of the tables with his coffee, he thought about the 'ghost' of Rose Cottage. Anthony Shepherd had claimed that his wife had always been very healthy. He couldn't understand why she should have died so suddenly. Yet he had known she was in hospital. He hadn't mentioned how he knew that.

Darren decided to put the supposed ghost's story to the test. He had no idea what it might lead to, but if Tony was right, at least he would know their conversation wasn't entirely a product of his imagination. He didn't know anything about Susan Shepherd after all. He had even heard her name from Tony first. If there really was something to his story—well, a little curiosity wouldn't do any harm, besides shortening the waiting time. He would try to find out whether Susan Shepherd had really died here in the hospital and whether her death was unexpected. He might even learn what the cause of death was.

As he wasn't a relative of the deceased, it wouldn't be easy to get at any information, but he would try his luck with a bit of charm. Even better that it gave him an excuse to talk to the pretty nurse at reception.

Now he just needed a way in. Darren looked around and pondered how to start a conversation about a dead woman he didn't know. As he glanced at the cafeteria counter, he had an idea.

A chocolate muffin in one hand and a caffè latte in the other, he approached the reception again. Fortunately, there was no sign of the grumpy patient. The nurse greeted him with a professional smile.

"How can I help you?"

Darren grinned. "Not at all." He pushed the muffin and the coffee cup across the desk. "I just wanted to say thank you."

"What for?"

"For taking such wonderful care of my grandma before she died."

The nurse's smile faded and gave way to an expression of regret. "My condolences. What was her name?"

"Sue. Susan Shepherd. She was such a wonderful lady." Darren looked mournful.

"She really was." Nurse Beales, as it said on her name tag, nodded. But then she looked at Darren suspiciously. "As far as I know, Susan didn't have any close relatives."

Crap. He had completely forgotten about that. But at least he had confirmed that she had been here and that she probably died here too. Nurse Beales obviously remembered her.

He quickly corrected himself. "I'm not really her grandson. Actually, she is—sorry, was—my great aunt, but she always let me call her Granny Sue. Unfortunately I was abroad until recently, so I hadn't visited her for quite some time. I suppose I'll always regret that now. I still can't really believe that she's gone."

"I see. I'm very sorry." The nurse looked at him sympathetically. Then she hesitantly reached for the chocolate muffin Darren had brought. He could see how much she wanted to take a bite. "She really mentioned me?" she asked to make sure.

Darren swallowed. Don't lay it on too thick now, he thought to himself.

"To be honest, no. But I know what a good job you're doing here."

As she looked up at him in surprise, he quickly added, "All of you, I mean."

Now she smiled. "So do the others all get a chocolate muffin too?"

Darren grinned guiltily. "Now you've got me. I also wanted to have a wee chat with you. I'm Dan by the way. Dan Shepherd."

She smiled. "Katie Beales." Then she cast a questioning glance at the coffee cup between them.

"A latte," Darren quickly explained. "To go with the muffin."

Katie nodded and pushed coffee and muffin aside. Then she propped her elbow on the counter and rested her chin in her hand. Her grey-green eyes sparkled at him. For the first time he noticed that she had freckles.

"So, now that we've established that you're trying to bribe me, what's this really about?"

Darren had to bite the inside of his cheek to make himself concentrate. Katie was really cute, but that's not why he was here.

He looked at her sheepishly. "To be honest, I feel a bit guilty."

Katie nodded. "I see. And how do you expect me to help you with that?"

"It's about my granny, I mean, great aunt. I'm afraid I didn't look after her enough. Even though she was so old."

If she asks me Susan's age, I'm screwed, he thought. But Katie simply nodded.

Darren hesitated. "I was wondering whether you could maybe tell me what she actually died of?"

Katie immediately straightened up and a look of disapproval appeared on her face. "I can't do that. It's against the rules."

"I know. I'm sorry. It's just that—perhaps she would still be alive if I'd visited her more often. Maybe I should have noticed that something was wrong." He hung his head, peeking up at Katie with puppy eyes.

The expression in her green eyes softened a little. "I don't think you need to worry about that. She was just old.

And old people die. That's just how it is, sadly. Even if we often don't want to accept that."

Darren nodded dejectedly. "But still. She'd always been such a healthy woman. I visited her only…" He wondered how long Rose Cottage had been empty. If he chose the wrong time now, he would be found out. Better to pick a conservative estimate. "I visited her last summer. She seemed perfectly healthy then."

Katie sighed. "But I can't."

"Please. There isn't anyone else I could ask."

Finally, the pleading look from Darren's brown eyes softened her. "Alright, then. I'll have a look. But not a word to anyone. I could lose my job for this!"

Darren pressed his lips together and ran his fingers along them as if he was zipping them shut. "Not a single word. I promise."

While Katie searched for Sue's file on her computer, Darren grinned inwardly. He never thought this could be so easy.

"Ah. Here it is." The nurse fiddled nervously with a strand of hair while she was reading the information on her screen. "It says cardiac arrest. Nothing unusual for a woman her age. I don't think there was any way you could have helped her."

Darren nodded sadly. Then he thought of something. "Can you tell me why she was here in the first place? Wouldn't it have been much more likely that she'd die of that at home?"

Katie tapped on her keyboard again. "She called 999 herself. She didn't feel well and complained about chest tightness and dizziness. When she arrived here, she was diagnosed with cardiac arrhythmia."

"So she had a heart problem?"

"Apparently." Katie shrugged. "I really can't tell you any more than that."

Darren smiled. "Thank you. Honestly, I'm sure you are right. There was nothing I could have done. I'm genuinely relieved."

They looked at each other uncertainly.

"Would it be completely out of order if I invited you to dinner as a thank you?" Darren asked.

She laughed. "Probably. What if I have a muscle-bound boyfriend with jealousy issues?"

Darren's smile faded. "Do you?"

She laughed. "No. But you should have seen the look on your face."

"How about tomorrow then? I'll pick you up after work and we can go to Markie Dans?"

Katie hesitated. She was just about to agree when she noticed an old lady standing behind Darren watching them. "Hello Mrs Bagshaw. Is there anything I can do for you?"

Darren wheeled round. His grandmother was standing right behind him.

"Hello Katie. I see you've already got to know Darren."

Katie's gaze turned from her to Darren. "You know each other?"

Darren smiled uncomfortably and tried to surreptitiously signal to his grandmother, but she continued undisturbed. "Of course we know each other.

This is my grandson, Darren. Didn't the rude oaf introduce himself?"

Katie raised her eyebrows in surprise. But it only took her a moment to regain her composure. She glared at him while she spoke kindly to his gran, "Oh, of course he introduced himself. But it seems I didn't quite catch his name properly."

Darren looked down. "Sorry," he mumbled.

Katie ignored him. "If there's nothing else I can help you with, Mrs Bagshaw, I'm needed on the ward."

She took the chocolate muffin and the untouched latte and dropped them into the bin. Then she gave Darren one last devastating look and stormed down the corridor.

Granny Erica looked after her perplexed. "I've never seen her like that. What have you done, Darren?"

He just shook his beetroot-coloured head and mumbled something incoherent. He hoped his grandmother wouldn't need to return here anytime soon.

After dropping his grandmother off in Ganavan, Darren drove over to Rose Cottage in Pennyfuir. He'd had enough of this entire episode. It was time to find out once and for all how the illusion of the old man was created. There had to be some trick to it, and there had to be a reason. Even if there was something in the suspicions of the supposed ghost, why of all people would anyone want him, Darren Bagshaw, to investigate Susan Shepherd's death? The whole thing was mystifying.

It was early afternoon when he arrived at the cottage. The sun was shining on the heath surrounding the hamlet and the sea sparkled in the distance. Good. No wires, projectors or speakers would escape his search in this bright sunshine.

When he looked over to the Stickle house, he saw the curtains behind one of the windows twitch. So Mrs Stickle was on the prowl again. He didn't care. He was hunting ghosts today.

He grabbed his equipment from the boot of the car: a powerful torch he had packed especially for this trip, a screwdriver for prising open possible hiding places, and his phone so that he could take photos if necessary. He checked that the phone's battery was charged. Then he was ready.

Darren regretted that he didn't at least have one of those wire detectors from a DIY store. Not because he believed that he could measure the ghost's energy, but because he thought the power lines could help him track down the location of speakers or other devices. The EMF meters that some ghost hunters favoured were utter nonsense. Where did they even get the idea that ghosts would create electromagnetic fields? Probably from Egon Spengler, PhD, he smirked.

First, Darren checked the living room and the two bedrooms. As was to be expected, there was no sign of the ghost in broad daylight, but he couldn't find any hidden speakers, lasers or other gizmos either. The old radio in the living room emitted some eerie noises when he switched it on, but that was because it wasn't properly tuned into a station. Darren didn't think that the ancient device had anything to do with the ghost of Tony Shepherd.

Next, he investigated the hallway. He switched on the light and opened all the doors to make the room as bright as possible.

"Tony? Anthony Shepherd?" Darren felt stupid calling for a dead man in an empty house, but if anyone was playing silly games with him, he wanted them to believe that he was falling for their ghost story.

There was no reply.

Darren systematically searched every nook and cranny. He even fetched a chair from the kitchen to check the top edges of the door frames for hidden wires. Nothing. Darren didn't know whether he should be relieved or disappointed. He had neither seen the ghost today nor found any installation that could have been used to create the illusion of a ghost. But he had seen and heard something here the night before. He surely hadn't imagined it.

When Darren was just about to leave, he heard a rumbling from one of the bedrooms. As he went to investigate, there was a voice that seemed to come from the wardrobe. "Young man?"

Darren slowly opened the wardrobe door a crack, and there he was. The old man was sitting on a shoe rack in the dark, looking at him curiously.

Darren immediately opened the door completely.

"No!" the old man howled—and disappeared.

Irritated, Darren searched the open wardrobe. He shone his torch into every corner, but apart from the shoe rack the wardrobe remained empty.

He had barely closed the door when he heard a low thump, like wellies on a wooden floor. This time he opened the door only a crack, and there he was again. Tony Shepherd.

Right, Darren thought. Time to try something else.

He closed the wardrobe and activated the voice recording function on his phone. Then he put it in his pocket. He would have liked to take photos or videos too, but he didn't want to frighten off the 'ghost'. The audio recording would have to do for now.

When he was ready, he opened the wardrobe door a little and gave the purported ghost a friendly smile. "There you are! I've been looking for you."

Tony eyed him grumpily. "I got the impression you were looking for something else altogether. Do you often climb the kitchen table or inspect the top of cupboards when you visit friends?"

Darren blushed. "Oh, that. I was just doing a bit of dusting."

"I see." The old man looked at him. "Did you at least find out something?"

"Actually, yes. Well, a little bit—but first I've got a few questions for you."

"What do you want to know?"

"Where do you go when I open the wardrobe door?"

Tony looked at him, confused. "I don't really know. Maybe I dissolve, no idea. But I could only ever visit my Sue when it was dark outside."

"Nobody could see you except your wife?"

"We've already been through this. No. Only you and the cat next door. Is that it?" The old man seemed impatient today.

Darren thought about it. "I think so. For the moment anyway."

"So, what did you find out? What was wrong with her?"

Before he could reply, a thought occurred to Darren. "I was told she called the ambulance herself, so she must have been here. Then why don't you know what was up with her?"

Tony averted his eyes and shifted uneasily on his shoe rack. "I wasn't here."

"Why not?"

"Because it happened during the day."

"So how do you know she'd gone to hospital? I don't imagine she called you from there."

"Of course not! She left me a note."

"Oh, I didn't think of that." Darren felt stupid, but in an era of smartphones and the internet, who would think that someone could just scribble a message on a piece of paper?

Tony fidgeted restlessly on his shoe rack. "Now tell me what you found out, please."

"Not much, to be honest. She was taken to hospital because of dizziness and chest pains."

Tony nodded and motioned for him to continue.

"When she arrived there, they diagnosed her with cardiac arrhythmia. She apparently suffered a cardiac arrest soon after."

The old man stared at him. "What? Just like that? There had never been anything wrong with her heart!"

Darren shrugged. "I'm sorry, but that's all they could tell me at the hospital."

Tony shook his head. "It doesn't make sense. She was always healthy and never had any heart problems. No high blood pressure or any other trouble with her circulation either. Yet suddenly she drops dead? She sometimes joked how she would survive her doctor, even though he was twenty years younger than her. Did they find any reason for the arrhythmia? Maybe she was poisoned."

It was Darren's turn to shake his head. "I don't know whether they found out anything else. I was glad someone told me as much as they did. But I don't expect the doctors looked at her very closely afterwards. After all, she was old, and many old people die of heart attacks."

"But not Susan!"

Tony jumped up and glared at Darren. The way he had to crouch inside the wardrobe, he looked like the clothes rail was sticking out of both his ears. It was rather disturbing. Even though the ghost or illusion or whatever he was obviously didn't notice.

"Please calm down."

"I don't want to calm down! Someone killed my wife and I want them brought to justice!" He looked pleadingly at Darren.

Darren sighed. "Even if that was true, who'd have a reason to poison her? Besides, wouldn't you have noticed?"

Tony looked down at his wellies, embarrassed. "Not if it happened during the day," he said quietly. "Please, you're the only one I can talk to. You have to help me."

Darren went quiet. This was getting weirder by the minute. He had come here to prove that Tony was a projection, that there was no ghost at Rose Cottage. Instead, the ghost now demanded he investigate an alleged murder, the death of the ghost's wife.

"Who would have had a reason to harm your wife?" he asked eventually.

As he posed the question, an image popped up in his mind: the nasty neighbour. The Shepherds' garden had obviously been a thorn in her side for a long time. But to kill someone because of that? And why now? If she had wanted to, she would surely have found a way to get rid of her neighbours years ago. Or she could have tried to get a court order to force them to keep their garden in order.

Tony shook his head helplessly. "I don't know. Sue was such a kind soul." He went quiet for a moment, scratching thoughtfully behind his ear. To Darren, it looked as if the clothes rail sticking out of his skull was itching. Eventually Tony looked at him. "There was this estate agent who was rather keen on our home. Libby something. Sue talked about her once or twice, but I can't imagine she would have poisoned my wife because of that. I can't think of anyone else."

Darren sighed. "Maybe we should find out whether your wife actually was poisoned before we start suspecting anyone," he suggested. At the same time, he realised that this would hardly be possible. Especially after he had fallen out with the pretty nurse.

Tony looked at him hopefully. "So you'll help me?"

Darren stared into his dark eyes. A little voice in the back of his head asked why the old man's problems should be any concern of his. Ghost or not, he barely knew him. Nevertheless, he felt responsible, even though he couldn't quite explain why. He nodded. Then he reached out to the ghost and they shook hands. The clothes rail still sticking out of Tony's ears spoilt the occasion somewhat, as did the fact that his hand didn't really exist. Then again, the whole affair was completely absurd anyway.

Darren shook his head in disbelief when he was sitting back in his car a short while later. Darren Bagshaw, private investigator for the departed. He still wasn't entirely convinced that he had actually spoken to a ghost. On the other hand, he had no other explanation for Tony's existence. But if Anthony Shepherd was real, Darren would be the first to possess a genuine audio recording of a ghost.

Grinning, he pulled his phone out of his pocket and started to play the recording of his conversation with Tony. He listened.

"There you are! I've been looking for you."

Pause.

"Oh, that. I was just doing a bit of dusting."

Pause.

"Actually, yes. Well, a little bit—but first I've got a few questions for you."

Pause.

"Where do you go when I open the wardrobe door?"

Irritated, he switched off the recording. What was that supposed to mean? Why had it only recorded his own voice? Maybe it was time to ask his grandmother about ghostly apparitions. After all, she seemed to believe in them, and perhaps Grandpa Alan had given her a tip or two on the subject.

But first he needed a break. And a beer!

CHAPTER 14

The Haunted House, Ganavan's old pub, was picturesquely situated above the beach at Ganavan Bay. There were a few sturdy tables in front of the pub, with a great view of the nearby islands. In summer, guests could enjoy their pints in the evening sunshine, while behind them the otherwise grey stone facade glowed in soft pink.

Now in April, it was still too cold and windy for that. Turning up the collar of his jacket, Darren hurried to get inside. Whitewashed walls, old oak beams, dark wooden tables and a few ancient photographs created the cosy pub atmosphere that the summer tourists loved so much. But it was also a place for the locals. A few regulars were already nursing their pints.

Only after he had settled down at one of the tables at the back with his beer, Darren realised the irony of his situation. After his experience at Rose Cottage, he had fled to the *Haunted House*, of all places.

Annoyed, Darren shook his head and took a sip from his pint. He was fed up with other people's superstitions. Ghosts did not exist, and no amount of wishful thinking would change that. Eventually he would find an explanation for Tony, the ghost of Rose Cottage. It was only a matter of time. Maybe hallucinogenic mould spores had spread through the empty house. Or Tony might just be some weird friend of Susan Shepherd's. Although Darren wasn't sure why he should want Darren to investigate the poor woman's death. Or how he managed to disappear when light fell on him. Nor did he have an explanation for the trick with the clothes rail sticking out of his head.

"Oi, Chubby Cheeks! Shouldn't you be looking after your grandmother?"

The burly figure of Greg Gudgeon towered over Darren's table. The old man was looking down at him disapprovingly.

Darren frowned. "She's fine. Norma and Janet are with her. She told me earlier they wanted to come round." He didn't know whether they actually did, but he thought it likely. In any case, he saw no reason to justify himself to Greg.

There was immediate understanding in Greg's rugged face. "So the witches' coven is in session? I see why you did a runner." Not waiting for an invitation, he took a seat at Darren's table and regarded his near empty pint. "I bet you needed that. You know what? The next one is on me."

Darren nodded gratefully. He didn't want to talk to Greg about his grandmother and her friends, but neither did he want to keep racking his brains about Susan Shepherd.

"Do you know why this place is called The Haunted House rather than The Green Man or The White Hart or whatever, like other pubs?" he asked.

Greg raised an eyebrow. "Are you wondering if it's worth setting up your ghost traps here?"

Darren forced a smile. Then he shrugged. "No, I was just curious."

The old man eyed him doubtfully. "You really don't know?"

Darren shook his head. He hesitated, then frowned. "Strange. Now you mention it, there is something. It had a different name when I was wee, right? I never thought about that."

"Well, if that is all you know, we'd best put that right straight away."

Greg signalled to the bar. "Haw, Pete! Two more pints, please. And young Master Bagshaw here would like to know why your pub is called The Haunted House."

Pete, the barman, eyed Darren with interest, although he frowned at being asked to bring the beer to the table. It was customary for pub-goers to get their drinks from the bar. But the name Bagshaw had obviously piqued his curiosity.

When he joined them at their table, he brought three pints.

"Are you related to Al the Seer somehow?" he asked Darren.

Darren frowned. "Should I know who that is?"

"Was," Greg corrected. Turning to Pete, he added, "He's Alan Bagshaw's grandson."

Pete's eyebrows shot up. He looked at Darren more respectfully. "So can you see ghosts too?"

Darren eyed Pete suspiciously. "What do you mean? There are no ghosts."

Greg sighed. "Told you, he doesn't know the history of the pub. Neither does he know about Alan's secret gift. Yet young Darren here works in Edinburgh as a ghostbuster. I'm sure if you have any spiritual problems, he can help you." He smirked.

"I'm not a ghostbuster!" Darren huffed. "I do ghost tours for tourists. Well, I did."

"So, you only asked about the Haunted House for your job?" Pete seemed disappointed.

The allegation caught Darren out. He opened and closed his mouth a few times without any sound coming out. "Absolutely not! I don't even do ghost tours anymore. For all I care, you can sod off with your ghost stories. It's all nonsense anyway. Can't a man just enjoy his pint in peace?"

Greg threw Pete an amused glance, then put a hand on Darren's shoulder. "Give us a break, laddie. I thought you'd be interested. After all, you asked. By the way, your grandad Alan was involved in renaming the pub." Turning to Pete, he said, "Why don't you just tell us the story?"

Pete's expression suggested he didn't think Darren was worthy of the honour. But then he looked at Greg and sighed. "Ach, I might as well, I suppose. I need to get back in practice anyway, what with the tourist season starting soon."

Before he began, he took a good swig from his pint and made himself comfortable. Despite his misgivings, Darren was curious to hear the story.

"It all began on a stormy night around twenty years ago. Old Al was a regular here then. The weather that night was so wild, none of the fishermen could head out to sea. Incidentally, the pub was still called The Haven back then. Not the greatest name, but not a bad one either, considering it was a good place to sit out a storm."

Darren nodded. The Haven. That was the name his grandmother still sometimes used.

"Anyway, Al had a bit more to drink than usual, what with the weather and nobody heading out to sea for another day at least. Then suddenly he leans over the bar and asks, 'Doesn't she get on your nerves sometimes?'

"I asked him who he was on about. 'That woman,' he said.

"I grinned. 'The missus? Of course. That's why we're getting divorced.' I had only just gotten rid of Tessa and all her frilly cushions.

"But old Al shook his head. 'Not her. *That* woman', he said, pointing upstairs and rolling his eyes conspiratorially. 'I'd sure go mad if I had to listen to her whining every night.'

"There was something funny in his voice when he said that. But of course it was nonsense. There was no woman living in the pub at the time. Especially not one who was always whining. I'd have had her out in no time!"

Pete took a sip from his beer and looked at Darren meaningfully.

He grimaced. "That's it? That's your amazing ghost story? It's not very spooky."

Pete nodded thoughtfully. "I'd say the same if that had been all. But from that day I started hearing things too. Not the whining, and certainly not every day, but enough to get me worried about my sanity."

Darren decided to play along. "What did you hear then?"

"Well, steps, and sometimes moaning."

Darren shrugged. "It's an old building, of course there'll be noises."

Pete nodded. "Aye. That's what I thought. Until one evening I heard an awful racket from upstairs. There was screaming and caterwauling and thumping all over the place." The old barman shook himself. "It was the screaming that did it for me. It was worse than a pig being slaughtered. Kind of human, but much creepier."

"What was it?"

"No idea. I didn't dare go upstairs and have a look. Instead, I went to get old Al. He had somehow started it, after all. I asked him if he could still hear the woman. When he said yes, I told him to go upstairs and make it stop. He didn't want to at first. He told me that's why he had become a fisherman, so he wouldn't have to deal with the spirits of the dead anymore. There are no ghosts at sea."

"Only on the Ship of the Dead," Greg muttered.

Pete nodded slowly. "Aye, only on the Ship of the Dead."

Darren frowned. "What are you talking about now?"

But Greg shook his head. "That's a different story, laddie. It doesn't belong here. Come on, Pete, tell him the rest."

The barman looked at the sea outside. He had gone very quiet since the Ship of the Dead had been mentioned, but Greg's prompting seemed to wake him from his memories. "Alright then. So after some negotiation, I managed to convince your grandad to go up to the attic, even though he obviously wasn't keen. He was up there for quite a while. I heard his footsteps and his voice, as if he was talking to someone. When he came down, he looked very tired, but content. He told me to get the stairs to the attic repaired, because the fifth step had a big hole in it. It had been like that forever, because I hardly ever used it. There was nothing up there, since I had enough room for everything in the cellar. I didn't need the extra storage space upstairs. But Al insisted that once the stairs were repaired, the ghost of that woman would shut up. She was just unhappy about the hole."

"What happened next?"

"What do you think? The whole story seemed fishy to me. I mean, there are some strange things in this world, and I've seen enough of that myself. But this? I was sure old Al had made something up to get the month's worth of free drinks I had to promise him."

"That's how much he talked you out of?" Greg seemed impressed. "Did it work?"

Pete shifted uncomfortably on his chair. "It did. The following nights were quiet. Nevertheless, I did some digging afterwards, as there was rather a lot of whisky at stake. There was a guy from Oban, who was interested in old houses and stuff like that. He agreed to help me."

"What did he find?"

"Well, that was the craziest thing ever. Turned out what Alan had said was true."

"What was true?"

"What he had told me about the stairs. A long time ago, maybe hundred and fifty or two hundred years ago, this house belonged to a fisherman. He must have been quite well off, as he owned not one but two boats. Nevertheless, he went out to sea himself every day, and whenever he was out there, his wife would go up to the attic to keep an eye on him."

Darren rolled his eyes. "Seriously? The White Lady who is consumed with grief for her lost husband? Isn't that a bit trite?"

Pete looked at him. "Do you want me to finish the story? Then hear me out. It wasn't quite that simple, by the way."

Darren blushed and nodded.

"The woman must have been quite the nag, because as soon as her husband returned, she'd demand something from him. Money for linen or a new dress. Or she urged him to do repairs around the house. She would always find something to pester him with. Some said that she didn't climb up to the attic out of longing for her husband, but to check on his catch. To make sure she'd get all the money off him."

Darren shook his head in disbelief.

"Eventually the staircase to the attic started to wear out. No wonder what with her tramping up and down every day! She wasn't exactly a pixie either. So she was on at her husband about getting the stairs repaired. But he brushed it off. Maybe he was hoping the dangerous climb to the attic would put her off watching him quite so closely.

"Be that as it may, he kept putting it off until one day, she saw his boat entering the harbour, started down the stairs and broke through a step. When he came home, he found his wife lying at the bottom of the stairs. Her back was broken, but she was alive, albeit barely. With her last breath, she swore she'd haunt this house until he repaired the broken step."

"What a weird curse." Darren frowned.

"Why? The dying probably have all sorts of weird thoughts, don't you think? As do the living, for that matter."

"But why would she still haunt the pub after so many years? I mean, repairing the stairs isn't that big a deal."

Pete nodded. "Aye. But that was plain bad luck. He certainly meant to get it done. It's a fine house after all. I guess he wouldn't have wanted to share it with her nagging ghost. But before he got round to it, he had an accident. What with all the chores his wife had kept bothering him with, he had neglected to look after his boat properly. Only two days after she died, he snuffed it too!

"He and his men were hauling in the nets. A rope broke, whipped across the deck, and pulled him into the water. When they fished him out, he was already dead. His men later swore they had heard his missus laughing. 'Serves you right, miser!', she's said to have shouted, but the fishermen probably made that up."

"So you believe my grandfather saw the ghost of this woman?"

Pete shrugged his shoulders. "Who knows? It certainly got quieter after I had the broken step repaired. Whether it was really necessary to put a bottle of whisky in her window once a month, I'm not so sure. At any rate, it was never there for long, so she must have drunk it."

Greg nodded solemnly. "Presents of whisky or rum to appease ghosts is an old tradition, not just in Scotland—by the way, do you still do that?"

Pete grinned. "You'd like that, wouldn't you?"

The old man shrugged but didn't seem particularly disappointed. "No harm in asking. Do you know, did she really have such big tits?"

"Who?"

"Your ghost. The pub sign has a rather well-endowed lady in a flimsy nightie."

"Oh, that. I'd call it artistic license. Besides, the tourists appreciate an attractive ghost."

"Oi, Pete! Are you still serving drinks today?"

The call from the bar made Pete get up. "Alright, alright, I'm coming."

"Do you believe it?" Darren asked after Pete had left.

"What?"

"My grandfather seeing ghosts. Maybe he was just a bit of a show-off. Or mad. Or both."

Greg shrugged. "I don't know. He certainly was a bit odd, but he didn't brag about seeing things. He sometimes called it a curse that ran in the family. I thought that's why you went to Edinburgh and became a ghost hunter."

Darren shook his head. "That must have been coincidence," he claimed, although he wasn't quite so sure anymore. Not for the first time, he wished he had known his grandfather better.

CHAPTER 15

When Darren arrived home, his grandmother was just taking a huge cottage pie out of the oven. Her walking stick was a few steps away and she was swaying under the weight of the dish.

Darren rushed to help her.

"Careful, it's hot!"

He quickly grabbed a tea towel before they manoeuvred the heavy dish to the dining table together.

"How did you manage to get that into the oven in the first place?" he wondered. The smell coming from the pie made his mouth water. The golden crust of mashed potatoes and cheddar cheese looked delicious.

"Don't ask!" Granny Erica replied, grinning mischievously. "Now let's eat."

Darren put plates and cutlery on the table. Then his grandmother shovelled generous portions of pie onto each of their plates. When they had finished, Darren made tea. Only then did he find time to contemplate the events of the day.

"Could you tell me about Grandpa Alan?" he asked.

His grandmother scrutinised him. "Yes, of course. Is there anything in particular you want to know?"

Darren shrugged. "I was in the Haunted House, and Pete the landlord was telling a funny story."

Granny Erica laughed. "The one about the White Lady? Your grandfather was rather proud of his idea."

Darren's eyes widened in surprise. "But Pete said he consulted a historian, who confirmed the story."

"It was a set-up," Granny Erica explained with a smirk. "Alan knew the man and told him exactly what he was supposed to 'find out'."

"So it was all just a joke? He couldn't really see ghosts?"

Darren was grinning too now. It was reassuring that his grandfather had only been playing tricks on his mates. Even though it didn't help him with his problem at Rose Cottage.

His grandmother suddenly became serious. "Yes, your grandfather could see the spirits of the dead, some of them anyway. But he never made a big deal of it."

"So why the ghost story?" Darren frowned.

"What do you think? He couldn't pass up the chance for free whisky and beer. His 'historian' got a share, of course. But it was also to make light of the ghost thing. The haunted pub was a good laugh—nobody really took that seriously. It was worse when he saw dead friends or neighbours. He never wanted to talk about that. Nor to be considered a nutcase."

"I see." Darren heaved a sigh.

Granny Erica looked at him worriedly. "What's up? Have you seen a ghost as well? Your grandfather always believed that you had inherited his talent. He said it would show eventually."

Darren shrugged his shoulders and avoided her gaze. "I might have seen something strange. But that doesn't mean I'm going mad, does it?"

"No. Seeing something you can't explain to yourself doesn't mean you've gone mad. Do you really believe it was a ghost?"

"I don't know. Probably not. But after what you've just told me, I'm not sure anymore." He looked at his grandmother pleadingly.

"How about you tell me what's happened? But maybe you should put something stronger than tea on the table first." She pointed at the cupboard where Darren had always nicked her homemade biscuits from when he was little. "Have a look in there. There should be some left."

After a bit of searching, Darren retrieved a bottle. "Tobermory twelve years," he read from the label. Not exactly the cheapest of whiskies. He looked at his grandmother quizzically.

Surprisingly, she blushed. "It was a present from Greg."

"Uncle Greg gives you whisky?"

"He brought it along on my birthday," she defended herself. "Now will you just pour us some please?"

Darren smiled. Judging by the level of the amber-coloured liquid in the bottle, Uncle Greg and Granny Erica had already had a taste of it. He filled their glasses with two fingers of whisky and placed a small jug of water on the table. He rarely drank anything other than beer, but he appreciated a nice wee dram every now and then.

He added a splash of water and toasted his grandmother. *"Slàinte mhath!"*

"Do dheagh shlàinte!" she replied, as tradition demanded.

"Not bad," Darren declared after taking a sip.

Granny Erica nodded. "Now tell me what you've seen."

Darren told her about the old man, the fruitless search for hidden wires and speakers, and what Katie Beales had told him at the hospital.

His grandmother smiled. "Ah, that's why she was so annoyed with you. No wonder. I don't think you handled that well at all, because she's a lovely lass. Besides, you could have warned me."

Darren shrugged. What was done, was done. Finally, he played the recording of the conversation he had with the ghost of Anthony Shepherd in the afternoon.

"Do you see why I'm worried I'm going mad? The guy disappears when light hits him, and I couldn't even record his voice on my phone. He was talking normally, not whispering or anything. What am I supposed to do now?"

Granny Erica nodded thoughtfully. Then she pushed her whisky glass towards him for a refill.

"I think we should ask your grandfather for advice," she announced when the glass was back in front of her.

Darren stared at her. "Are you away with it already after the one wee dram?"

She smiled. "I'm not the one seeing ghosts here. If you think you can manage on your own…"

"So how do you think Grandpa Alan is going to help me? He's dead!"

His grandmother's eyes twinkled. "Could you fetch the oil lamp and light it please?"

When that was done, she switched off the electric light.

"Alan? Are you here?" she asked into the gloom.

Darren stared at her. "What's that supposed to be? A séance? Can you see ghosts now too?"

"No, but maybe you can," she replied with a grin. "Have a look around. Can you see him anywhere?"

Darren shook his head. Nevertheless, he scanned the darkened room. As you'd expect, nothing. He raised his glass to his lips. He probably needed more whisky to see ghosts here in his grandmother's living room.

But hang on. What was that? Was there a shadow on the Orkney chair? As he looked more closely, the dark outline became clearer. A moment later he recognised his grandfather sitting in the armchair and grinning at him.

Darren's jaw dropped. "Gran..., Grandpa Alan?" he stammered.

Granny Erica banged the table excitedly. "I knew it. You can see him, right?"

"How did you know that? Did you put something in my glass?" He eyed his beaming grandmother suspiciously. "Do you see him too?"

Granny Erica's smile faded a little. "No. I only see him in my dreams, although sometimes I can feel his presence in our home." She looked at the armchair where the ghost of her husband was sitting. "I'm glad you're here, Alan. I miss you."

The ghost's gaze softened. "Please tell her I'm very sorry I left her so soon," Grandpa Alan said.

Darren stared at him. Then he pulled himself together and passed the message on to his grandmother. Even though he was probably hallucinating, that seemed the least he could do.

She smiled bravely. "I know, my dear. Today you need to help your grandson though."

Grandpa Alan looked at him expectantly.

Darren ran his tongue over his lips. "Are you really a ghost?" he asked. He felt a bit stupid to be asking that.

His grandfather smiled. "What else could I be?"

"I have no idea. A projection, perhaps, or a hallucination. After all, there's still no proof that ghosts exist."

Grandpa Alan nodded. "That's true. So you think I'm a hallucination?"

Darren considered that. "Not really," he admitted eventually. "How could I talk to you, if you weren't here?"

He looked at his grandfather. Short-cropped white hair, a weather-beaten face, a thick dark-grey Aran jumper, a pair of strong hands, brown trousers and chequered slippers. He looked exactly like Darren remembered him. Maybe he was a figment of his imagination after all?

Baudrons the cat had entered the room and was staring at Grandpa Alan. Then he jumped up into his lap, or at least where the old man's lap should have been. The fat cat fell straight through him and landed on the seat. It didn't seem to bother Baudrons though. He curled up as if he had really landed on someone. When Grandpa Alan started stroking him absent-mindedly, he purred.

Shaking his head, Darren focused on his grandpa's face again. "Why can't Granny Erica see you? And why couldn't I see you while the light was on?"

Grandpa Alan shrugged. "To be honest, I don't know. The thing with the light is simple enough—it's too exhausting to make myself visible when it's bright. But why some people can see ghosts while most can't? I'm not sure. Maybe it's something to do with their brain waves, or maybe their eyes can see parts of the spectrum that others can't."

Darren immediately shook his head. "It can't be that. Ghost hunters have tried infrared and ultraviolet cameras and all sorts of other things, without ever capturing the image of a ghost."

"Then it will probably remain a secret how it works." Grandpa Alan didn't seem particularly concerned.

Darren pondered before asking, "You say it's too exhausting to make yourself visible when it's light. Does that mean you spend your days hiding invisibly in a corner eavesdropping?"

The old man grinned at that, revealing a row of pearly white teeth in his weather-beaten face. "Of course not. I rest during the day. I can't really explain it—just imagine that I switch to a different plane of existence or something like that for sleeping. A bit like you going to bed and dreaming."

Darren nodded thoughtfully, but he did find it rather difficult to imagine.

"Right, so what's the problem you wanted to talk about?" his grandfather asked.

Darren shrugged. "I've met a ghost. Or at least someone who claims to be a ghost. Looking at you here, he might well be telling the truth. It was over in Pennyfuir. His wife died recently, and he wants me to find out why. He believes that she was poisoned."

His grandfather nodded. "I assume he can't leave this world until that's been cleared up, right?"

Darren frowned. "I hadn't even thought about that yet. He didn't mention anything."

"Still, that's what it'll be. There's always some problem with moving on to the afterlife when ghosts turn to a seer." Grandpa Alan heaved a long-suffering sigh. "For us, that usually means nothing but trouble. That's why I went to sea. You get some peace there."

Darren was lost in thought.

"You didn't promise him anything, did you?" his grandfather asked.

"What? No, I don't think so—well, maybe I did. I told him I'd find out if his late wife was poisoned."

Grandpa Alan sighed. "I reckon you better do that then."

"Why?"

"Because he can haunt you if you don't. If you break your promise, he can follow you anywhere, like a curse."

"Doesn't he have to stay in the house he is haunting?"

The ghost shook his head. "Not if there's a broken promise he wants to avenge."

Darren grinned uncertainly. "You're pulling my leg, aren't you?"

"Unfortunately not."

"What's up?" Granny Erica asked. She had only heard one side of the conversation of course.

"I'm cursed!" Darren announced and rested his head on the table.

"Cursed? How do you mean?"

Darren ran his hands through his short hair. "Grandpa Alan says I'm cursed because I gave a promise to a ghost. He says the ghost could haunt me anytime and anywhere until I make good on the promise."

"You mean, your ghost could just appear here in my kitchen?"

Darren looked at his grandfather. When he nodded, Darren nodded too.

Granny Erica looked around as if she expected to see him right there.

"Although maybe he doesn't yet know he can do that," Grandpa Alan interjected.

"Maybe he doesn't know yet," Darren repeated for his grandmother.

She nodded, somewhat reassured, and shrugged. "It seems you should fulfil your promise as soon as you can then."

"But I don't know how!"

Granny Erica rested her head in her hands. "That does sound like a problem. Do you really have no idea? What exactly are you supposed to do for him?"

Darren shook his head. "I promised Tony I'd find out if his wife was really poisoned. But how am I supposed to do that? I'm not a doctor, and she was buried months ago."

His grandmother nodded thoughtfully.

Eventually Grandpa Alan cleared his throat. Or rather, the ghost of Grandpa Alan. It was amazing how quickly Darren forgot that his grandfather was actually dead. The ghost sitting in the armchair in the gloom seemed so lifelike.

"Does it matter how the lady was poisoned?" he asked.

Darren looked at him confused. "How do you mean?"

"Your ghost likely only cares that the culprit is punished."

"Quite possibly. But how does that help me?"

"It's very simple. Instead of trying to find out how she was poisoned, concentrate on who might have done it, and for what reason. Once you know the killer, you'll probably also find out how he or she did it."

Darren nodded slowly. "That sounds quite logical. If there is a killer in the first place. Who'd want to kill an old woman?"

Granny Erica grinned. "Fortunately, I'm always reading detective stories, and what I've learned is that only love, sex and money are sufficient motives for murder."

"Granny, please. This isn't a crime novel. And what's with the sex? The lady was well over seventy. She lived on her own. I can't imagine sex is worth considering as a motive here, especially with her husband haunting her home. Besides, there are other possible motives, for example revenge and rage."

Granny Erica folded her arms. "If you know better, go and look for your suspects by yourself. But I tell you one thing: a raging killer wouldn't use poison. That's far too slow. He's more likely to become violent."

"Okay. Not rage then. But what use are the motives to us?"

Granny Erica shook her head in disbelief. "Have you never watched a murder mystery? We just think through who might have each motive—let's start with love. Who could have a reason to kill her for love?"

"How am I supposed to know that? I never even met her. Who knows if she left behind a string of broken hearts when she was younger or whose marriage she may have ruined?"

"I don't think we'd have to go back quite that far. Wasn't there anyone more recent?"

"You mean apart from her ghostly husband, who might have felt cheated, what with being so dead and alone?" Darren's eyes suddenly lit up. "Could a ghost poison someone?"

"No," Grandpa Alan replied.

"Besides, why would he ask you to find the murderer if he'd done it?" Granny Erica added.

Darren's grin faded. "You're right. I guess we can exclude Tony Shepherd as a suspect then." He scratched his head. "The only other man I can think of is Uncle Greg."

"Greg Gudgeon? What gave you that idea?"

Darren shrugged. "A neighbour said he'd been visiting Susan regularly. I thought maybe he had a bit of a crush on her. You know he's been a bit lonely since his wife died."

"Hmm," said his grandmother, glancing into the corner where her husband's ghost was sitting. "Maybe there's another reason behind that. He's quite a talented handyman. Last year he helped Janet with her leaky roof, and he repaired the shower at Norma's."

Of course, Darren knew that Greg also liked to visit his grandmother. He was a bit of a charmer and of course he was a gentleman. A ladies' man, as Aunt Norma had once described him. Besides, he was always willing to help. Whenever he was needed, he was there, although Darren wasn't sure what his grandfather made of Greg inviting himself for tea at his grandmother's so often. Judging by the look on his face, he wasn't entirely pleased.

"Do you really believe Greg could kill someone?" Granny Erica asked doubtfully.

Darren considered that. "With the right motive, I think anyone is capable of murder. But Greg killing a woman? He'd be more likely to kill the postman. Speaking of which, the postman had been visiting her too."

"How is that surprising? Everyone gets post sometimes."

"But according to the neighbour, Birtwistle often stayed quite long, even when he didn't have any letters for her."

"Really? How would she know that?"

Darren got the impression that this information surprised his grandmother more than that Uncle Greg had been visiting Susan Shepherd regularly. He shrugged. "Excessive nosiness, I assume. Do you think he might have poisoned Susan?"

"Andrew a murderer? I can't imagine that. In any case, what reason would he have? I very much doubt he was in love with her. He must be more than twenty years younger than Sue. She probably invited him in, and he just wanted to be polite."

"The neighbour thought he might have hoped to inherit something. Well, Uncle Greg might have. She thought Birtwistle was just lazy."

"What an outrageous gossip that woman is. Somebody ought to teach her some manners!"

"That may be so. But an inheritance can't be the motive anyway. Certainly not for those two, because the house and everything else went to her nephew."

"Good point," Granny Erica agreed. She seemed relieved she didn't have to think about Greg's and Andrew's love lives any more. "That takes us straight to the next motive. What about money? Who did benefit from Susan Shepherd's death?"

Darren thought about it. "Her nephew. She didn't have any other heirs that I know of. Apart from that, maybe Libby. I'm sure she'll get a sizable commission for selling the house. Apparently, she'd been quite keen on it too. She'd already approached Sue about selling it."

"But how was she supposed to know that the nephew would sell the house? And even then she couldn't be sure the nephew would pick her as his estate agent."

Darren shrugged. "I'm not saying she's a murderer. I just wanted to note that she gains from it. That only leaves revenge as a motive."

"Have you got somebody in mind? Who'd have had anything against Sue? And why?"

"Well, obviously I don't know who Sue Shepherd might have angered during her life. According to her husband, she was the nicest woman in the world and had no enemies. But what else would he say? To me, the neighbour seemed somewhat suspicious. The one who'd been spying on her I mean. She didn't seem to mourn Sue Shepherd's death one bit. Quite the opposite. She was hoping to get new neighbours who would tackle Sue's overgrown garden, which was endangering her perfect lawn."

"You believe Sue Shepherd was murdered by her neighbour because she hadn't been mowing her lawn?"

Darren shrugged. "Why not? It wouldn't be the first time that an argument between neighbours turned deadly. Often, the reasons seem completely trivial to outsiders."

"Fair enough. Is there anyone else we should add to our list of suspects?"

Darren pondered. "The neighbour mentioned a lady from the Women's Institute, who'd visit Sue sometimes. Marcy or something like that. I don't know what her motive would be though, unless Sue always beat her to first prize in the cake competition. Perhaps the neighbour just wanted to distract me from her own motive."

"Right, so we have the money-grabbing nephew and the vengeful neighbour as our main suspects. Then, Libby, the commission-hungry estate agent, Greg, the charmer hoping for a bequest, and Marcy, who might have been jealous about a cake recipe. Andrew was there as well, but he didn't really have a motive."

"Nice summary, but what do I do now?"

"Very simple. You need to have a closer look at each of our suspects, and of course you have to make sure we didn't miss anyone." Granny Erica yawned. "But not today. Or at least not with me, because I'm going to bed."

Soon after, Darren was sitting alone at the table. His grandfather's ghost was still hovering over the armchair in the corner. Darren rubbed his eyes and looked at him.

"How did you feel when you first saw a ghost, Grandpa? Did you also think you were going mad?"

His grandfather smiled. "Aye, it was rather strange, but it was easier for me. I knew straight away that the person I saw was dead."

"Why?"

"He was a dockworker. There was an accident. A rope snapped and decapitated the poor man."

Darren's eyes went wide. "You saw it happen? How gruesome."

"No. Fortunately, I wasn't there for the accident. But you could tell what had happened from looking at the ghost."

"How? Was he carrying his head under his arm or something?"

"Yes, something like that, but it was a long time ago and I'd rather not think about it."

Darren nodded thoughtfully. "Will this happen a lot now?"

"What?"

"That I see ghosts. There are so many people. And some of them die every day. There must be thousands everywhere."

His grandfather shook his head. "Fortunately, it's not that bad. Most of the dead go straight to the other side. The others stay here for a reason. Often they're just waiting for their loved ones. They rarely need your help. But better try pretending you can't even see them. Then they won't think to ask you for help."

Darren nodded, although he wasn't sure how else he could have responded to the old man approaching him at Rose Cottage.

CHAPTER 16

When Darren woke up the next morning, the first thing he saw was the whisky bottle on the table. There wasn't much left in it. A developing hangover confirmed his assessment—he had too much to drink last night. Even though he was sure he had only poured himself one or two more drams to mull things over after his grandmother had gone to bed.

Had he really been talking to his dead grandfather about ghostly apparitions? And had he discussed murder suspects in the Sue Shepherd case with his grandmother? He didn't even know whether that lady really had been murdered. The only person convinced of that was the ghost of her dead husband. And even he hadn't actually seen anything suspicious!

Darren groaned.

A steaming mug floated into view. It smelled Christmassy.

"Here. Drink that."

He turned his gaze from the mug to his grandmother, who stood beside the sofa wide awake and in an absurdly cheery mood.

"What is it?" he asked, carefully taking the mug from her.

"Tea with ginger and lemon. It'll do you good."

He tried a bit and pulled a face. "Can't I just have a coffee?"

"You can have one when you've finished that."

Darren grumbled, but sitting wrapped in his blanket on the sofa was clearly better than getting up and making his own coffee. He obediently drank his tea and waited for Granny Erica to bring his coffee.

But when he had finished the tea, she shooed him to the bathroom instead. "You've got to hurry. Libby called. She's already waiting for you."

"Libby?" Darren squinted at his phone in confusion. It didn't show any missed calls. That could only mean she had called the landline phone that was in Granny Erica's bedroom. He shook his head. He had to stop this.

Half an hour later, Darren was sitting in the car. After a shower, a coffee and a quick breakfast of eggs and toast he felt slightly more ready to face the day.

Darren was to meet Libby at her office. As Maggie's car had broken down, he needed to fetch the keys from Libby and fresh bed linen from the laundry. After that he would pick up Maggie, so they could go and clean the two holiday homes together.

When he arrived in Oban, Libby was rearranging the adverts in her window.

"What's that?" he asked in amazement as he saw the photo she had prominently placed in the centre. It showed a manor house as big as a small castle, with more turrets and protrusions than he had ever seen on any other house. The upper floor had wooden beams and tiny windows, like a timber-framed Tudor house. Downstairs, huge windows dominated the façade. Some of them even had colourful stained glass.

The estate agent grinned. "Cameron's Folly. Most recently a hotel. Do you like it?" Then she furrowed her brow. "I wonder whether it will find a British buyer. Most houses at that price level are bought by foreign investors these days."

Darren was still admiring the photos of the mansion. It had fifteen bedrooms, apparently. "Does it have a resident ghost?"

Libby gave him a questioning look. "What makes you say that? Do you think a ghost would increase the price it'll fetch? Maybe you're right. Speaking of ghosts, how are you doing with Maggie and our other haunted houses?"

He shrugged his shoulders. "That hasn't been a problem again."

She raised an eyebrow in surprise. "Really? I'm glad to hear that. Maggie's superstitions do make me worry at times. I wouldn't like to lose her, but she's scared away new staff with her horror stories before. Anyway, I'm glad you're such a grounded guy and don't believe in ghosts."

Darren nodded, relieved she didn't ask any further questions. But talking of ghosts reminded him of Tony Shepherd and his remark about the estate agent who wanted to sell Sue's home.

Looking at Libby, he could well imagine that she was working hard for her success. Maggie had said that she was one of the most successful estate agents in Argyll. But would she commit murder just to get her hands on a property to sell? That seemed a bit far-fetched. At least for such an insignificant property.

"What's the current owner of Rose Cottage like?" he suddenly asked.

"Craig Clough? He's alright. Why do you ask?"

Because the ghost of Anthony Shepherd believes that his wife was murdered. Darren had to stifle a grin. Better not go there. Instead, he looked at her innocently. "Just curious. It's a cute little house. I wondered why he doesn't want to keep it, especially with the constantly rising property prices."

Libby gave him a quizzical look. "Are you trying to ruin my business?" Then she shrugged. "I think he just doesn't want the bother. He's got a thriving business down south, so I don't think he really needs the money. But looking after a house so far from home probably is too much hassle for him."

Darren nodded. "Do you mind if I keep the keys for a few days? I'd... I'd like to tidy up the garden a bit more."

The estate agent eyed him sceptically, but then shrugged. "If you like. But if I find you've moved in or you're throwing parties, I'll deduct the rent from your wages."

He grinned. "Deal!"

When Darren arrived at Maggie's flat after collecting the laundry, she was already waiting impatiently. She looked gorgeous as always, even in the old T-shirt and ripped jeans she was wearing for the job.

"I didn't want to hang around here all day! I've got better things to do!"

That comment was enough to bring Darren back down to earth. They were colleagues, nothing more, as Maggie had made quite clear on their first day. He rolled his eyes and beckoned her to get into the car.

They worked quickly and quietly in the two holiday homes. This time Maggie didn't make Darren continue on his own after she had finished her part of the work.

"What's bugging you today?" she asked when he was taking the dirty linen to the car, deep in thought.

Darren realised he hadn't exchanged more than a few words with his colleague all day. "I'm sorry, my head's just so full."

Maggie put her arms on her hips and looked at him defiantly. "Are you implying my head is empty?"

Darren looked at her, confused. It took a while for the penny to drop. Then he blushed. "I…, I didn't mean it like that," he stammered.

"Yes, you did. You're one of those men who think women are stupid!" Maggie accused him.

Darren shook his head vigorously. "Quite the opposite!"

"Really?" Now she was grinning at him. "Prove it. Tell me about your problem. Is it about a woman?"

Darren hesitated. Would it be a good idea to involve Maggie in his investigation? Then again, why not? It wasn't like he was doing anything illegal. Maybe she could help him somehow.

He nodded. "You're right, it's about a woman."

Maggie's eyes lit up with curiosity. "Your girlfriend? Have you got heartache? Or are you looking for a romantic present? I'm sure I could help with that."

Her enthusiasm made him grin. "No, it's not about my girlfriend, but an older woman. She's at least seventy."

Maggie gave him a funny look. "Do you fancy old ladies? Or is this about your grandmother?"

He shook his head and laughed. "Neither. In fact, the lady in question is dead."

Now Maggie looked completely confused. "Why do you need a present then?"

He wondered how much he should tell his colleague. He would certainly keep quiet about the fact that he had seen a ghost. But how else could he explain why he was interested in Susan Shepherd?

"No. I'm, erm, just doing some research. For Libby."

Maggie's eyes narrowed. "For Libby? What's in it for you then? And why didn't she ask me?"

Darren was floundering. "Well, it's kind of a test. And no, there's no money in it. Maybe next time, if I do a good job."

Maggie crossed her arms in front of her chest and glared at him.

He hastened to add, "Of course, I'll tell her that you helped. And I'm sure next time she'll have a job for you too." Darren was sweating. He wondered how he was going to talk Libby into this, when he didn't even know if it was worth dragging Maggie into his investigation. His little fibs were getting out of hand.

Maggie seemed happy enough though. "Alright then. What is this about?"

Darren collected himself. "Do you know Rose Cottage?" he asked.

Maggie shrugged. "Which one? The one in Gallanach or the one in Pennyfuir?"

Darren frowned in surprise.

"What? It's not like Rose Cottage is a very distinctive name."

He nodded. "Pennyfuir."

Maggie wrinkled her nose as she tried to remember it. "Is that the one that looks like ABBA's weekend getaway inside?"

Darren grinned. "Exactly!"

"But I thought this is about a woman?"

"It is, in a way. What do you know about the house?"

Maggie leant against the car. "I think I've only been there the once. Libby had just added it to her portfolio, and the house clearance company was there."

"Then why is all the old furniture still there?"

"Probably because a house is easier to sell when it looks homely."

"I see. Did you notice anything unusual during the clear-out? Inside or around about?"

She pondered. "Not really. It was all just junk that the clearance guys were chucking out. What should I have noticed?"

"The people. Any suspicious characters?"

Maggie laughed. "In Pennyfuir? It's nothing but suspicious characters there."

"Please!"

"Alright." Maggie closed her eyes. "To be honest, there wasn't much going on. A few neighbours came out to gawp, and the postman dropped by. Nobody else that I can remember."

"Nothing unusual then?"

Maggie shook her head. "Some of the neighbours were a bit creepy."

"Which ones? The Stickles?"

She looked at him blankly.

"The ones next door, with the manicured lawn."

Now she nodded. "That could be them. There was a couple. She was wearing a tweed two-piece, and he an expensive-looking golf sweater. You'd have thought they owned a country estate rather than a poxy little bungalow."

"What did they do?"

"That was creepy. They were grinning happily, as if they were glad the old woman was dead. And there was me thinking that English people are so polite and well-mannered."

"Scottish," Darren corrected automatically. "But I see what you mean. Anything else interesting?"

Maggie shrugged her shoulders. "Not much. They wouldn't stop going on about their garden. I think they wanted to persuade Libby to get rid of that big tree behind the house. They got quite upset when Libby told them she had no intention of doing that. When they realised she wasn't the new owner, but only the estate agent, they calmed down, but I reckon the people who buy the house will have something to look forward to with that pair."

Darren nodded thoughtfully. "Do you think they could be dangerous?"

"How do you mean?"

"I mean, do you think they would harm someone because of their perfect lawn?"

"You think they might have bumped someone off, like in a horror film?" Maggie giggled. "Nah, seems unlikely. They didn't look like people who'd get their own hands dirty. Maybe they'd get their lawyer involved. Although, if you went and dug holes in their beloved lawn, I could imagine the husband coming after you with a hedge trimmer. Why do you ask?"

Darren shrugged. "No particular reason. I just wanted to know what you thought about the neighbours."

Maggie shook her head. "Seriously, I wouldn't want to live next to them. Far too stressful."

"Thank you," Darren mumbled while thinking.

After a couple of minutes, he noticed her watching him. "What?"

"That was it? I thought you were going to tell me something about an old woman?"

Darren sighed. "Another time, okay? I've got enough for today."

Maggie shrugged. "Alright, but remember you owe me if Libby pays you anything for your research. Now, please drop me off at the garage. I hope my car is ready."

CHAPTER 17

That evening, Granny Erica and Darren sat at the dining table chatting for a long time. Grandpa Alan didn't show up this time, but the thought that Darren could now see ghosts and that he was helping one of them seemed to have inspired his grandmother. While he had been at work, she had spent her time making inquiries.

She had dug up a few stories about the Stickles, who apparently guarded their property jealously. A cousin of Granny's friend Janet had once been abused and threatened by them because her terrier had left a little deposit on their lawn. After she had picked up the mess, they still demanded twenty pounds compensation, which the terrified lady paid just to get away from the pair.

Granny Erica hadn't found out much about the other suspects though. Susan Shepherd's nephew apparently lived quite far away, and nobody could remember when he had last visited. Marcy, the lady from the Women's Institute, had a reputation for compulsive helpfulness.

"Her children have flown the nest, and now she mothers any old people who don't slam the door on her quickly enough, Norma claims. She was surprised she hadn't tried it with me yet."

"She's probably heard what an independent and stubborn woman you are," Darren suggested.

"Quite possibly." Granny Erica grinned. Then she suddenly frowned. "I wish I had the cast off, so I could go for my daily walks again. But at least I've got something interesting to do now, thanks to you."

Darren didn't respond. While he was grateful for his grandmother's help, he was getting a bit tired of spending so much time thinking about the Shepherds.

Fortunately, his grandmother soon noticed how late it was. She retired to her room, leaving Darren and Baudrons on their own.

At breakfast the next morning, Granny Erica announced that she needed to go to the hospital again.

Darren looked at her with concern. "Is something wrong?" Even though she didn't seem any worse than the evening before, he was worried that the last few days had been a bit much for his grandmother. While she was still quite fit, she was no spring chicken anymore.

But Granny Erica smiled. "I'm fine. I just need to talk to someone."

Darren quickly called Libby to let her know, then drove his grandmother to Oban. After parking the car in front of the hospital, he hesitated. He wasn't keen on facing Katie Beales again after what had happened last time.

"Do you mind if I wait out here?"

His grandmother shook her head. "I'm sure I won't be long."

In fact, she was back after a few minutes. She smiled like the cat that got the cream. "I hope you haven't got anything planned for tomorrow night, because you've got a date," she announced as she got back in the car.

Alarm bells went off in Darren's head. "Please tell me you didn't do that!"

She looked at him innocently. "What do you mean?"

"I want you to tell me you haven't embarrassed me even more in front of Katie Beales."

"I wouldn't do that, and you've done quite enough of it yourself."

Darren didn't know whether he should feel relieved. "So, you didn't talk to her?"

"Yes I did, to apologise on your behalf. To make up for it, you're inviting her to the Corran Halls tomorrow night."

"She agreed to that?" Darren was amazed.

A happy grin spread across Granny Erica's face. "Of course she did—although admittedly she didn't have much choice. After all, she's a nice girl and was brought up with Highlands courtesy."

Darren frowned in confusion. "What's that got to do with it?"

"I told her I'm part of the warm-up act at the concert tomorrow and that I'd be very happy to see her there. She couldn't say no to that."

"She believed you?"

"Why wouldn't she? The Vatersay Boys will be playing. They won't mind if I and a few friends play a piece or two first. Who knows, maybe we'll even do one together."

Darren sighed in resignation. When his grandmother got something into her head, there was little point trying to resist.

"Why do you even care if I make up with Katie?" he asked instead. "Do you think I couldn't find myself another girl if I wanted to?"

His grandmother looked him in the eye. "That too, but mostly I was thinking it would be good to have someone with medical knowledge to help us with the Sue Shepherd case."

Darren looked at her stunned.

"As far as I'm concerned, we can go home now," his grandmother remarked, and looked out the window. Her self-satisfied smile spoke volumes.

Shaking his head, Darren started the engine.

That afternoon, Darren met up with Maggie in Benderloch. He had intended to have another look around Rose Cottage and talk to the ghost of Anthony Shepherd, but Maggie had called to ask him for help with the creepy converted church. Darren grinned. His opportunity for revenge had finally arrived.

They went inside together. Even though it was still light outside, Maggie seemed nervous.

"Are you sure you don't mind doing the upper floor again?" she asked. "After everything that happened last time?"

Now that he knew her better, Darren could see how her eyes were sparkling, despite her nervous demeanour.

"No problem."

He wondered whether she had prepared some more scares for him. In any case, she seemed disappointed by his relaxed attitude.

While Maggie was fetching something from her car, Darren hurried into the downstairs bathroom to set up the first part of his plan.

When he heard his colleague come back into the house, he hung his jacket over the banister and stomped upstairs, making sure she knew where he was.

Darren looked around to see what needed doing, while at the same time listening out for what Maggie was up to. Judging by the clatter, she was busy cleaning the kitchen. That meant it would probably take a while until she found his little present. He quickly started dusting in the bedrooms, hoping to finish before anything happened downstairs.

When he heard Maggie getting the rubbish bag ready to take outside, he took a break from his work. As soon as she had passed the bottom of the stairs, he crept into the kitchen. This was where the second part of his revenge would begin.

He had just got everything ready when he heard a gurgling giggle that seemed to come from the pantry. A quick look inside showed that it was empty. Probably those old pipes again, he thought. Then he had to hurry to get back upstairs before Maggie returned.

He bumped about a bit to reassure her that she was alone downstairs. Then he waited.

After about two minutes, he heard Maggie go into the bathroom. He quietly crept onto the landing and peered down. Suddenly he heard a scream followed by a thump. Then Maggie came running out of the bathroom, slamming the door behind her. Darren grinned.

Of course he rushed down the stairs to help, putting on a concerned face when he found her pale and breathing heavily in the hall.

"Everything alright? What happened?"

Maggie stared at him wide-eyed. Darren took her by the arm and led her towards the kitchen. It wasn't until they were sitting at the kitchen table that she found her voice again.

"There's a body in the loo," she whispered hoarsely.

Darren allowed himself an indulgent smile. "A whole body? How is that supposed to fit in there?"

Maggie shrugged her shoulders impatiently. "No idea, but there's a head. I saw the eyes. Horrible." She shook herself.

He nodded slowly, as if he thought she was overreacting a bit.

As expected, Maggie glared at him angrily. "You don't believe me?"

"Of course I do."

Darren's soothing tone only made her angrier. "Go and see for yourself then!" she urged him.

That was just what Darren had been waiting for. "Okay. You'll want to make yourself a cup of tea in the meantime. I'm sure it'll make you feel better." With a clunk, he switched on the shiny espresso machine before leaving. Now he could only hope that she'd take the hint and make herself a coffee instead of tea.

He went to the bathroom and lifted the toilet lid. A pair of bloodshot eyes stared back at him. They really looked quite convincing. Darren had to admit that the sales assistant in the shop had been right, they definitely were worth the higher price. The water they were floating in was milky white and moving a bit, which made it look like the eyes belonged to a real face. Grinning, Darren fished them out and hid them.

"There's nothing here," he shouted towards the kitchen before flushing the remaining evidence down the toilet.

When he left the bathroom, he heard a clatter from the kitchen. Immediately afterwards, Maggie bolted down the hall like the Devil himself was after her. She was pale as a ghost.

"Get me out of here!" she panted, hiding her face against his shoulder.

Grinning, Darren wrapped his arms around her. But she was shaking so much that he really had to take her outside. He steered her to a bench in the garden and sat down next to her.

Despite the sunshine, it took a surprisingly long time for Maggie's breathing to calm down. She let go of his hand and gave him a sideways glance. After watching him carefully for a while, she frowned.

"You did that, didn't you?"

"What?" Darren tried hard not to look smug and to feign honest interest.

She gestured at the house. "The body in the loo and the blood coming out of the coffee machine."

He looked innocent. "Why would I do something horrid like that?"

Maggie stared at the lawn and the trees. Then she sighed. "Alright, you win. So maybe I played a trick on you when we were here last time. Still, what you did today was a bit much." She looked at him reproachfully.

Darren shrugged. "I didn't think you'd be that scared," he confessed. "The blood from the coffee machine is just some red food colouring I put into the water tank. And you started it: the ghostly message on the mirror, the shoe polish on the door handle…"

Maggie waved it off. "You're right. Shall we call a truce?"

She told him why she had prepared those pranks for him. "It's a tradition. My predecessor did the same to me."

"But why?"

She shrugged. "For fun, but also as a test. If you can't cope with that, you really shouldn't work here. Some of the houses are seriously creepy."

Darren smiled. "Do you know the story about this one?"

She shook her head.

"Would you like the hear it?"

Maggie thought about it for a moment. "No, thank you. This house is spooky enough already."

Darren nodded. Maggie had a point. After everything he had experienced in the last few days, it no longer seemed impossible that there really might be a ghost in the converted church.

Maybe he should look for the ghost of Reverend Rees some time. If he found him, perhaps he could be persuaded to pose for a photo as the Poltergeist of Benderloch, so Darren could be the first to prove the existence of ghosts. But first he should talk to his grandfather again. He realised he had no idea how ghosts could get themselves noticed. He knew nobody else could see or hear Tony Shepherd, but not whether poltergeists were real.

Eventually they went back to work. They didn't talk about it, but they stayed together while they finished cleaning. They wiped the red stains off the kitchen floor and the coffee machine and finished Darren's chores in the upstairs bedrooms together.

The ghost of Benderloch might have been Maggie's own invention, but there was no harm in being cautious.

On the way home, Darren dropped by Rose Cottage again. He parked on the road and looked at the house. He wondered what he should tell the ghost. How would he ever find out if Sue Shepherd had been poisoned? And his list of suspects was rather questionable too.

The curtains at the Stickle house moved when someone came to the window to watch him. Suddenly Darren realised the absurdity of the whole situation. Libby was employing him as a cleaner, yet here he was playing the sleuth. If there really was something to investigate, he ought to leave it to the police.

But what would you tell them? A voice at the back of his head snickered. A ghost told you he believes his wife was murdered, yet the doctors in the hospital didn't notice anything? Oh, and your prime suspects are the neighbours, simply because they are compulsively neat and a little obsessed with their lawn.

Darren sighed. It was crazy. When the curtains at the Stickle house twitched again, he started the car and drove home.

CHAPTER 18

The next day was a Saturday. The tourist season hadn't started yet, so for once there were no houses waiting to be cleaned.

Darren enjoyed being able to have a proper lie-in for once, at least until his grandmother started getting out pots and pans in the kitchen. He pulled his pillow over his head and groaned. Although she hadn't particularly urged him to get up before, she kept Darren on his toes from the moment he left his bed. He didn't even know why.

Shortly after four in the afternoon, Granny Erica served an early dinner. At five o'clock she disappeared into her room, after telling him to be ready to go on the dot of six, and that he should put on something decent for his date with Katie.

He grumpily looked at himself. He was wearing black jeans and a black long-sleeved shirt. What more did his granny want? Black was always appropriate, wasn't it?

While she was getting ready, he put on a new, better-fitting pair of jeans after all. He also spent a good quarter of an hour brushing his short auburn hair into a meticulously dishevelled look.

Soon after, his grandmother emerged from her room. She had put on dark red lipstick and rouge. Her white hair was pinned up and decorated with some brightly coloured flower clips. He couldn't see what else she was wearing as she had wrapped herself in a long red chequered coat.

"Could you put my bagpipes in the car please?" she asked. Then she put several things, possibly makeup, into her handbag, before carefully getting into the passenger seat.

"Won't we be far too early if we leave now?" grumbled Darren.

But his grandmother shook her head. "It's always better to be there in good time for a gig, because of the sound check and the lights and so on."

Darren wondered how often she was performing in Oban. They reached the venue at the Corran Halls at half past six.

"Should I go and pick up Katie now?" Darren asked.

Granny Erica shook her head. "No, she'll be walking. She should be here any minute now."

As predicted, Katie appeared at the entrance to the building soon after.

"Wonderful!"

Darren's grandmother pointed at the case containing her bagpipes. "You take that, Darren," she ordered.

Then she let him help her out of the car. Using her crutch, yet surprisingly briskly, she led her two companions through the stage entrance and various doors into the hall where the event would take place. Of course, it was still empty this early before the start of the show.

"Make yourselves comfortable. It will start in a few minutes."

After Granny Erica had left them, the atmosphere in the big empty hall turned awkward. Darren fidgeted for a moment, before pulling himself together.

"I'm very sorry. I shouldn't have lied to you." He looked at his shoes while saying that.

Katie grinned. "That's okay. Your grandmother explained everything."

Darren looked up in surprise. "She did?" He wondered what new tale his granny had spun for Katie. Fortunately, he soon found out.

"Oh, yes. She said you often spent the summer in Ganavan when you were a kid, and that Sue Shepherd was almost like a second grandmother for you."

Despite his surprise, Darren managed to nod.

Katie shook her head. "Why didn't you just tell me?"

"Because—" Darren desperately tried to think of an excuse. Couldn't his grandmother have come up with something for that part as well? "Because of data protection," he blurted out. "I thought you were only allowed to tell her relatives about Granny Susan's medical records, and I didn't want to get you into trouble. Honestly."

He hoped he hadn't laid it on too thick, and that she hadn't heard the relief in his voice after inspiration struck him at the last moment.

Katie just shook her head. "You're right about the DPA, but we're all human. If I had known you were related to Mrs Bagshaw, I'm sure I would have helped you anyway."

Darren nodded dejectedly. He obviously should involve his grandmother more in his investigation. If he left the search for suspects to her, he could certainly save himself a lot of trouble. The only thing he felt uneasy about was that it might put her in danger.

"Is she really playing in the warm-up act today?" Katie asked.

"To be honest, I have no idea. I guess it'll be a surprise."

Darren offered to take Katie's coat to the cloakroom and fetch something to drink. She nodded gratefully.

When she took off her coat, he couldn't help but stare at the screaming colours, the pointed collar and the long cuffs of her blouse. She grinned. "That's an original. From my grandmother."

Darren nodded, lost for words, and wondered what other weird clothes might be lurking in her wardrobe.

When he returned to the hall without her coat, but with two pints of beer, he noticed that Katie was no longer the only one who was dressed so flamboyantly. Around half the audience were wearing flared trousers, loose-fitting blouses and colourful accessories.

Shaking his head, Darren handed Katie her pint and waited for the concert to start. When the room was a little more than half full, a man stepped onto the stage.

"Good evening, ladies and gentlemen. Before we get to tonight's main event, I'm delighted to introduce our local support act. Please give a warm welcome to the *Ganavan Antiques*!"

Darren grinned at the band name that Granny Erica and her friends had chosen, but his smile froze as he saw them walking onto the stage.

At the front, he recognised his grandmother. She was limping a little as she was still hampered by her walking cast, but she was wearing a long evening dress that he was sure he had never seen before. It must have been covered in sequins, because it sparkled in the spotlights as if it was made from black diamonds.

She was followed by a man in a brightly coloured shirt, who was wearing a huge pair of sunglasses. Darren was surprised to spot a clerical collar on the man's neck as he sat down at the drums.

"Reverend McEges?" Darren whispered to himself. He barely knew Ganavan's minister, but who else could it be?

Behind McEges, Pete, the owner of the Haunted House, took to the stage. He was wearing extra-wide flared trousers but looked quite normal otherwise. He had a bass guitar draped over his shoulder and was grinning and waving to the crowd.

The next band member surprised Darren even more. Unlike the rest of them, Greg Gudgeon was dressed as he always was. The burly old man didn't seem comfortable on stage, as Darren got the impression he was trying to hide behind his accordion. He wondered how his grandmother had managed to talk Greg into this appearance.

The last to take the stage was a woman Darren didn't know. Katie, on the other hand, was so shocked she nearly choked on her pint.

"That's Miss Lindsay," she explained. "She was my primary school teacher."

The teacher was at least twenty years younger than his grandmother. Darren wondered how she liked being one of the Ganavan Antiques.

There was a brief pause while the band were setting up. Then Reverend McEges set a rhythm and they launched straight into their first song. It took Darren a few beats to recognise the melody, as he had never heard the song accompanied by bagpipes or the accordion before. His jaw dropped.

"They're playing ABBA?" he whispered. He had only just collected himself enough to give Katie a shocked look when Miss Lindsay launched into the first lines of 'Dancing Queen' with fervour.

Katie grinned. "Of course. Didn't you know?"

Darren shook his head. He looked around the hall. Suddenly the strange outfit many of the audience were wearing made sense. But why would they dress up for the warm-up act? A suspicion arose in Darren's mind.

"Who's the main act today? It's not the Vatersay Boys, is it?"

Katie stared at him. "Are you telling me you didn't know it's Abbamania playing tonight? The show's been announced for weeks. I was surprised that Mrs Bagshaw had managed to get hold of tickets, but seeing how she smuggled us in through the back door, she probably didn't need any." She grinned.

Darren shook his head. An ABBA tribute band might not have been the entertainment he would have picked for his first date with Katie, but he had to admit the Ganavan Antiques were better than he would have expected.

When the main act began, you could really have believed that Agnetha, Björn, Benny and Anni-Frid had returned to the stage. Granny Erica had joined Katie and Darren after her performance, and they spent the next two hours singing along to ABBA songs with everyone else. Even though Darren wasn't a big fan, he found he knew the words to many of their songs anyway.

About halfway through the show, he suddenly thought he spotted a familiar figure in the crowd. Someone who couldn't possibly be here. He excused himself and pushed his way through to the other side of the hall.

There, in the shadows to the side of the stage, stood Anthony Shepherd. Or rather, his ghost, which Darren was reminded of by the fact that he disappeared every time a stage light briefly shone in his direction. As usual, he was wearing a sun hat, dungarees and wellies. But why the hell was he here?

When the ghost recognised Darren, he smiled shyly. At the same time, he looked a little worried.

"What are you doing here?" Darren snapped at him. He really didn't want the ghost to spoil his evening with Katie.

Instead of answering, Tony Shepherd looked around curiously. "Where are we? I didn't know time travel was possible now."

Darren frowned. "It's not." Then he gestured towards the stage. "We're in Oban. They're just a cover band."

"Oh. Of course." Tony smiled embarrassedly. "I probably should have known that, but I've been dead so long and haven't been out in a while. This place looks almost like back when my dear Sue and I used to go dancing."

Darren nodded impatiently. "Why are you here?"

"What? Oh, right." Tony looked uneasy. "Am I interrupting something? I just wanted to ask how you're getting on with your enquiries. Have you found out anything yet?"

"Yes. Well, a bit. But this really isn't a good place to talk about it."

Tony glanced around and nodded. "You might be right there."

Darren noticed that some of the audience were watching him curiously. Fortunately, they couldn't hear what he was saying over the loud music. Nevertheless, him talking to someone invisible must have looked rather strange. If he was lucky, they would only think he was drunk.

"Shall we go outside?" the ghost suggested.

Darren looked up to the heavens pleading for help. "No, we'll not go outside," he clarified. "I'm here with a girl." He didn't mention that his grandmother was there as well.

"Oh." Suddenly, Tony looked even more lost in the hall full of happily singing people.

Darren huffed. "Alright. I'll be at Rose Cottage tomorrow. We'll talk there, but now please get out of here. I don't have time for this tonight."

The ghost hung his head and nodded dejectedly. Then he faded until seconds later he had vanished completely.

Darren breathed a sigh of relief. Tony was right, of course. He really hadn't made much of an effort to find out more about his wife's death and the possible suspects, but now wasn't the time to change that.

To have some excuse for his sudden disappearance, he went to the bar to get new drinks for Granny Erica, Katie and himself. Then he rejoined them.

The rest of the evening passed undisturbed, at least from ghostly intrusions. After the concert, Granny Erica and most of the Ganavan Antiques moved on to Markie Dans, a nearby pub. Darren would have preferred to keep

Katie's attention to himself, but she seemed to be having a great time with the oldies.

Darren was the only one who wasn't in a good mood. It wasn't just the Antiques' presence and being limited to soft drinks as his granny's chauffeur, but also because of Tony Shepherd. While the others burst into beer-fuelled song, his thoughts repeatedly drifted back to the ghost.

Granny Erica eventually gave him a shove. "If you're only going to sit here trying to spoil everyone's mood, you might as well go home."

Darren shook his head. "It's alright," he claimed.

But his grandmother didn't give in. "You don't need to stay for me. The Reverend can take me home."

They looked across the table. The minister was on something like his fifth gin and tonic, and was just telling Katie a story that required vigorous gesticulation.

"Do you really think he should still be driving tonight?" Darren asked doubtfully.

Granny Erica waved dismissively "He could drive that route with his eyes closed. Besides, he's got divine assistance."

"As long as you're sure."

Darren was glad to get out of the noisy pub. He threw Katie a hopeful look. "Do you need a lift home?" he asked and pointed at the car keys.

She smiled at him in a way that gave him butterflies, but she shook her head. "No need. I haven't got far to go."

Darren looked at her and wondered if he could persuade her to have a coffee with him, but before he could open his mouth, Reverend McEges had grabbed her attention again.

"See you around then," he said to the back of her head. He waved at the others at the table and went on his way with a heavy heart. When he turned around one last time, he saw Katie's eyes on him. She seemed in a good mood and waved, but obviously she had no intention of following him.

As Darren walked back to his car through the chilly night, he realised he had enjoyed the evening, despite everything. He needed to have a serious word with his grandmother though. If she insisted on arranging a date for him, she should at least have the good grace to leave him alone with Katie.

CHAPTER 19

Back at his grandmother's cottage, Darren started thinking about the Shepherds again. Try as he might, he couldn't come up with a way to help the ghost. It was all too nebulous and there was little real information. The Stickles still were his prime suspects, but would the neighbours really have murdered poor Sue Shepherd because of her unkempt garden? It seemed rather far-fetched even to him.

The problem was he didn't know enough about the deceased. That meant he needed talk to people who had known her better. One was the ghost of her husband, obviously. But maybe Greg Gudgeon could help him too, if it was true that he had visited Sue regularly. He was a suspect himself, yet that was all the more reason to finally talk to him. Darren struggled to imagine Greg as a ruthless killer. Then again, weren't murderers often the ones who you least suspected?

He didn't learn anything interesting on his visit to Rose Cottage the next day. As it was daylight, he found Tony in the wardrobe again. The ghost confirmed that Sue Shepherd's nephew ran his own company. Tony didn't know of any financial problems, but he hadn't visited his aunt often.

Regarding the Stickles, Tony only repeated what Darren already knew. Yes, there had been a few arguments about the garden, but he didn't think they would get violent over it. Moreover, he didn't know of any recent reason why they should be upset with Sue. They were always complaining about someone or other anyway.

As if to confirm that assessment, only a few minutes earlier Darren had seen Mrs Stickle with a face of thunder, stomping over to their other neighbours, the family with the three children.

"Your disgusting mutt has left a deposit in our garden again!" she had shrieked. "If that happens one more time, I'll report it and have it taken away as you're obviously not able to control it!"

The mother had looked around anxiously, but apparently couldn't spot their dog anywhere. She had raised her hands apologetically and tried to calm Mrs Stickle.

Darren had only just parked his car outside Rose Cottage. He couldn't hear what the mother was saying, but he did see a small black and white dog. It was busy digging in one of the Stickles' decorative flower beds, probably hunting a mouse or a mole.

Darren briefly thought about shooing it away to save it from a cruel fate in an animal shelter. But then he thought that he would probably just draw attention to the wee scamp. So Darren went straight into the house to look for the ghost.

Now he could only agree with Tony Shepherd regarding Mrs Stickle. She wouldn't get her own hands dirty with murder. Not even by poisoning. She was the type to hire someone to do the dirty work for her. But hiring a professional killer over an argument with a neighbour? What for? A lawyer would be cheaper and had the advantage that the victim would know who had done them over.

After talking to the ghost for a while, Darren shook his head in frustration.

"For the life of me, I still have no idea who might have wanted to harm Sue or why. Perhaps she was ill, and you just didn't know about it?"

Yet the ghost was convinced, "She would never have gone and left me like this. I'm certain there wasn't anything wrong with her—she was very healthy for her age. That means someone must have murdered her. There's no other possibility."

"But who? She hardly ever had any visitors. Apart from her nephew, there were only Marcy from the Women's Institute, Greg Gudgeon and the postman. I don't know about anyone else. Do you really think one of them is a killer? Do you believe the postman murdered her, because… Well, why would he? She didn't even have a dog that could have torn his trousers. And I can't imagine the other two had any reason to harm her either."

Tony remained stubborn. "Susan didn't just die." Yet he had no suggestions either who might have killed his wife and for what reason.

Darren sighed, "Alright then. I'll have a chat with Greg. I know him, so hopefully he'll tell me some more about your wife. But if I don't find out anything from him, you'll have to accept that it was a natural death."

Tony Shepherd nodded dejectedly, although the glint in his eye suggested he wouldn't give up quite that easily.

Darren groaned inwardly. Was there any way he could withdraw from his promise? Maybe Grandpa Alan had some advice.

Greg's bungalow was just a short walk from Granny Erica's home. He looked surprised when he opened the door for Darren, but after a moment's hesitation, he waved him in.

Even though they had known each other for many years, Darren had never been to his home. No, that wasn't quite true. He had once spent a night at the Gudgeons' as a child. He couldn't remember why, but he did remember Greg's wife Sophie looking after him lovingly.

As Darren looked around the house, he could still see her influence, even though she had been dead several years. He had expected the house to have degenerated into a shabby bachelor pad, but it wasn't like that at all. The living room with its cream-coloured upholstery was bright and tidy. The old photos on the mantelpiece obviously got dusted regularly. There was even a healthy pot plant in the window.

Darren looked at Greg in surprise.

He shrugged his shoulders. "Sophie was always so proud of our home, and I don't have much else to do."

Darren nodded thoughtfully. "But you're helping Granny Erica and others in the village with repairs, aren't you? Granny told me you fixed her bedroom window the other day because it was getting stuck."

Greg waved dismissively. "I only do that so I don't get out of practice. I've got all the tools, and it would be a shame to just leave them lying around. Do you want a beer?"

He gestured to Darren to sit down somewhere while he went to the kitchen. Soon after, they were sitting on the sofa, cans of Tennent's in hand.

"I didn't realise you still played the accordion," Darren began, not wanting to immediately spring things on Greg.

"Aye, but only for myself." When he saw Darren's quizzical look, he sighed. "One of the Antiques couldn't make it, so your grandmother asked me to step in."

Darren nodded. "You really weren't bad. Why don't you join in regularly?"

Uncle Greg shrugged. "I don't like being on stage—now let's get to the point. Why are you here?"

Darren looked up in surprise.

"Och, come on, laddie. You never visited me before. And now you suddenly turn up on a Sunday afternoon to talk to me about playing the accordion?"

"Yeah, well…," Darren wasn't sure where to start. "You regularly visit my grandmother—" he eventually began.

Greg frowned. "What is this? Are you going to warn me not to break her heart or something?" He shook his head. "Erica and I are adults. We both know there won't ever be anything between us, but that doesn't mean I can't visit her for a cup of tea once in a while. And anyway, that's really none of your business."

Darren shut his mouth, which had hung open during Greg's outburst. He hadn't expected that the old man would be so clear-sighted about his relationship with his grandmother.

"No … well … actually, I wanted to talk to you about another lady you knew—Susan Shepherd."

Greg eyed him suspiciously. "Sue? Who told you that I knew her? And what's it to you anyway?"

Darren lifted his hand placatingly. "It really is none of my business. I just wanted to know a bit about her."

"Susan is dead. That's all there is to know. Why are you interested in her anyway?"

Darren thought about what he should tell Greg. In the end he decided to go with the truth. Part of it anyway. "I work for Libby Whatmough now. Aunt Norma's niece, the estate agent?"

Greg shrugged his shoulders. Then he nodded. "So?"

"She's been asked to sell Rose Cottage, and I wanted to find out a bit about the house and its last owner."

"What for? And why are you asking me?"

"Because you used to visit Sue Shepherd regularly, so I thought you could tell me a bit about her. After all, you knew her quite well, didn't you?"

Greg shook his head. "I still don't understand how this concerns you or Libby Whatmough."

Darren hesitated. What else could he say? What else should he say, he corrected himself. Besides, he had to keep in mind that Greg was still a suspect. Even though there was no motive and Darren couldn't imagine Greg poisoning anyone.

He took a deep breath. "Alright then. There's a suspicion that Sue Shepherd's death wasn't entirely natural. That she might have been poisoned."

"Poisoned?" Greg stared at him in disbelief. "Why would anyone want to poison Sue? And what on earth makes you think that?"

"I have no idea why anyone would have wanted to harm her. That's why I wanted to talk to you."

"Then where does this suspicion come from all of a sudden?"

Darren wondered if he could claim that the hospital had found irregularities in their data. But why would they approach an estate agent with that? No. He owed Uncle Greg the truth. "Somebody told me that she'd always been remarkably healthy. He thought it unlikely that she'd die so suddenly."

"Who said that? And why didn't he go to the police with it?"

"He couldn't."

"Why not?"

"Because it was her husband."

Greg looked at him uncomprehendingly "Her husband? You mean Tony? But he died years ago!"

Darren shrugged. "Exactly."

Greg stared at him. Darren could practically see the cogs working behind his forehead. Eventually he appeared to have alighted on the only possible explanation. "Are you telling me that you've spoken to the ghost of Anthony Shepherd?"

He laughed in disbelief, but Darren just looked at him.

Greg stopped laughing. "Is this because of the story that Pete told you in the Haunted House? About your grandfather being able to see ghosts? Are you trying to wind me up because of that?"

Darren shook his head. "That's nothing to do with it. I really can see ghosts. Well, one. Actually, make that two, as I've seen Grandpa Alan as well."

"Yet only a few days ago you were saying that it's all nonsense. I know you didn't believe us. You kept going on about those guys who expose fraudsters."

Darren shrugged. "Let's just say I refused to accept it at the time. Believe me, it was quite a shock."

"You're taking the piss!"

Darren sighed. "Could we put the ghost issue aside for the moment and concentrate on Sue Shepherd?"

"But even if I accepted that Tony's ghost told you he thought Sue was poisoned, I still don't see how that concerns you."

Darren closed his eyes and groaned. "Because I stupidly promised to help him, and until I make good on my promise, he can follow me anywhere. That's what Grandpa Alan said and so far I have no reason to doubt him."

Greg grinned and shook his head. "Well, I'll give you that, Chubby Cheeks, when you make up a story, you really think it through."

"Uncle Greg, please! I asked at the hospital. What they told me about Sue Shepherd's death really did sound a little strange. She called an ambulance because of chest pains, and a few hours after she got to the hospital, she died from a heart attack. Even though she never had any heart issues before."

"Aye, that does sound odd. But what are you expecting me to do?"

"You could help me find out who might have held a grudge against Sue. And maybe how she was poisoned, if indeed it was poison."

"Alright, I'll try. But I'm doing this for Sue and Tony, not because I believe your ghost story."

Darren shrugged his shoulders. "Whatever. Anything's fine by me."

"You've certainly got one thing right—Sue was remarkably healthy for her age. It really shook me when she died so suddenly."

"Was there someone she was having a fight with? Anyone who might have wanted to harm her?"

Greg thought about it for a moment, but then shook his head. "Not that I know of. She got along well with everyone. Her neighbours could be difficult sometimes, but nothing out of the ordinary."

"Did you notice anything unusual in the days before she died? Any threats? Maybe she hadn't been feeling well?"

Greg scratched his chin thoughtfully. "No, nothing. I gave it some thought of course after she died, but she seemed the same as always. Her arthritis had grown a wee bit worse lately, but she had a tea for that, which she swore by."

"What about that Marcy from the Women's Institute?"

"What about her?"

"She'd been visiting Sue. Was there anything unpleasant maybe? Any quarrels?"

"Surely not. Marcy can be a bit pushy, but she means well. She probably thought that Sue was lonely. But that's certainly no reason to kill anyone."

"So you didn't notice anything?"

"I'm sorry. No."

Darren sighed. "It seems her doctors were right then. There's nothing suspicious. She died because she was old."

Greg looked at him reproachfully. "You're going to make it that easy for yourself? One dead end and you give up?"

"What do you mean? It was you who said you didn't notice anything weird. And it seems nobody had any reason to kill Susan Shepherd."

"But you didn't know her. Now I come to think of it again, it's true that she died very unexpectedly. What if there really was foul play?"

"So what am I supposed to do? I've already spoken to the hospital and the neighbours. Granny Erica has asked around as well. There is nothing suspicious except that she never had any heart issues but still died of heart failure."

"Then maybe that's what you should look at next."

"What do you mean?"

"The poison. What could she have been poisoned with to trigger heart failure like that?"

"How am I supposed to know?"

Greg shrugged. "I have no idea, but maybe Erica does. She knows her way round herbs and that sort of thing, doesn't she?"

Darren sighed. "I'll ask her."

"Good lad. I'll think about it as well. Maybe I'll come up with something."

Darren nodded dejectedly. If his investigation continued like this, he could expect to have a nagging ghost in tow for the rest of his life. Unless Grandpa Alan knew a way to exorcise the ghost of Tony Shepherd. He no longer had much hope of finding out if and how Sue Shepherd had been murdered.

CHAPTER 20

Around noon the next day, Darren met Katie at the Costa Coffee in the centre of Oban. His grandmother had arranged the date after Darren had said his goodbyes in Markie Dans on Saturday night. Even though he was embarrassed about Granny Erica interfering again, he was looking forward to seeing Katie.

As the weather was fine, Darren got them two large takeaway coffees. A cappuccino for himself and a mocha for Katie. When he saw how much sugar she added to her cup, he grinned and asked if he should have got her a hot chocolate instead.

She threw him the suffering look of a martyr. "Have you ever tried their Black Forest Hot Chocolate and Cream? It's incredible. But I have to get back to work later, so I need the caffeine."

"Suit yourself. I'll just get us a couple of brownies then."

"You want me to get fat," she accused him. But when he tried to pick up the bag from the counter, she snatched it with a grin.

They strolled along the esplanade together until they found a bench where they could sit and watch the huge ferries depart.

"So, you're a proper ABBA fan?" Darren asked.

Katie laughed. "Not really, but it was fun anyway, don't you think?"

"Uh-huh."

No matter how much he had enjoyed it, Darren wasn't going to admit to more than that.

"Your grandmother is a very special woman."

"That's one way of putting it." He took a sip from his coffee.

"She told me you used to work in Edinburgh?"

Darren nodded. "For three years."

"How was it? I don't think I could ever live in a big city like that, but I imagine it's quite exciting?"

He shrugged his shoulders before realising how terse he was being. He smiled at her. "It was great. The pubs, the pretty students—I mean, well, the nightlife in general. Even the tourists could be fun sometimes."

"Your grandmother told me your job was something to do with ghosts. Are you a ghostbuster or something?"

Darren rolled his eyes, but grinned. "That's what she likes telling people. I think she just enjoys making fun of me. No, I was doing guided tours of the Old Town at night. You know, haunted houses, ghosts, stuff like that. Tourists love to be scared."

"Have you ever seen one? A ghost, I mean."

Darren hesitated briefly. Then he grinned. "Of course not. It was all just to entertain the tourists. There are no real ghosts. At least not in Edinburgh."

Katie looked a little disappointed. "Shame really. I imagine it could be quite fascinating. Just think of what a ghost from the eighteenth century could tell you."

"I don't know if I'd like to hear about that. Life in Edinburgh must have been quite hard. Hunger, poverty, and the internet wasn't even invented then. Imagine that!" He pulled a face as if that last one was the real horror.

Katie laughed.

"But even though our tours are for tourists, they are still interesting. You get to places you'd never see otherwise."

"What was the craziest thing you experienced on those tours?"

Darren didn't have to think long about that one. "The ghostbusters."

"You had ghostbusters? In overalls like Bill Murray in the films? And did they have magnetometers and ghost traps?"

"Sounds like somebody knows their stuff!" He grinned. "Actually, most of them only bring cameras and night vision goggles. And no, they don't wear overalls. They look quite normal really. But we had a dowser once. He was quite difficult to get rid of."

"Why did you want to get rid of him? Wouldn't it be amazing if you could prove that there really are haunted houses?"

Darren grinned. "Otherwise, yes. But he'd set his mind on a cellar where my boss had a little, let's say, installation. Of course he didn't want that to be found."

"So it was all just a scam?"

"No. Only in the one cellar. It wasn't anything particularly fancy either. He'd hidden a small fan in a pipe, to create a cold draft, and there were sound recordings I could switch on and off with a remote. No idea what was on there. It sounded like whale song or something. Anyway, the tourists were always impressed."

"Shame you had to help things along like that, but at least I now know where you learned to lie."

Darren's grin froze. "I'm sorry. I didn't mean to get you into trouble."

But Katie just smiled and hit him playfully on his arm. "Don't take it so seriously. It's okay, it was for a good cause."

She took a sip from her mocha and gazed pensively towards a fishing boat that was being loaded with lobster creels.

Darren looked at her with concern. "What's up?"

She shrugged. "I'm not sure, but what happened to Mrs Shepherd got me thinking. On my last night shift I browsed through some old patient records. She wasn't the only one where something like that had occurred."

"How do you mean?"

"That she suddenly died even though she never had any heart issues before."

Darren looked at her. "Are you saying this is normal?"

Katie shook her head. "No, I don't think it is. Yet in the last couple of years there have been at least three similar cases. All were elderly and had no relatives nearby."

"I don't understand."

"Me neither, but I'm a little worried."

Darren frowned. If there was more than one death, that would cast a very different light on the demise of Sue Shepherd. It certainly ruled out the neighbourhood dispute.

"Do you want to take the matter to the police?"

"What am I supposed to tell them? I'm only a nurse. If the doctors say it's all fine, then that's the way it is. Besides, I'd like to keep my job."

"Do you think somebody at the hospital might be involved?"

Katie shook her head. "I don't think so. It was different doctors each time, both in A&E and later on the ward certifying their death. Besides, what would a doctor gain from something like that?"

"What would anybody gain from poisoning old people?"

"I don't know. Their money? But they weren't related and I don't think they knew each other either. At least not all of them. Although they didn't live far from each other, as they were all from the area north of Oban, from Ganavan, Pennyfuir and Benderloch."

"Could you give me the list? Maybe I could find out some more."

Katie gave him a pained look. "Sorry, I can't do that. I shouldn't even have looked up the patient data myself, as I didn't have anything to do with their cases."

Darren nodded hesitantly. "Okay. But if you find Mrs Shepherd's death suspicious too, at least I've got a reason to keep looking for the culprit."

Her eyes went wide. "You think she was murdered?"

"Possibly. It seems unlikely that she poisoned herself before calling 999."

"Have you got a suspect?"

Darren shook his head. "Nothing made any sense so far, but if there are more deaths, then maybe this isn't just about Mrs Shepherd."

"I'll try to find a connection between the other victims."

"If you find something, please let me know."

"Of course."

Katie looked at her watch. "Oh, crap. My shift starts in twenty minutes, and I still have to dash home to get changed."

She said a quick goodbye. Darren pushed the bag with the brownies that had sat forgotten beside them into her hands. Then she hurried off with a happy grin on her face.

Darren sipped thoughtfully from his now lukewarm cappuccino. So it almost certainly wasn't the neighbours.

His phone rang. It was Maggie.

"Why aren't you here yet? Do I have to do everything on my own today?"

"What are you talking about? Where are you?"

"At the Attwood house, of course. Haven't you got Libby's message?"

"No. What's up?"

Maggie sighed audibly. "Just come here as soon as you can." She hung up.

The Attwood house wasn't difficult to find. It was a spacious cottage at Greenacre Bay on the Ganavan Road north of Oban. Darren had been driving past it almost every day when he went into town. Like all the houses in the small settlement, it had a wonderful view of the bay and Maiden Island.

As he pulled into the drive in his grandmother's Corsa, Maggie came out of the house.

"I didn't even know this place was for sale," Darren declared while looking around.

Maggie shrugged. "It's only just come in. The clearance guys were here this morning and now we're supposed to tidy up so Libby can start viewings."

Darren frowned and followed her into the house. "Clearance? Why didn't the last owners take their stuff with them? Or did they evict unruly tenants?"

Maggie rolled her eyes. "The previous owner was an old woman. Virginia Attwood. She's dead, which is why she didn't take the furniture. Her only relatives live in America, and they want the house cleared out and sold."

"Oh, right." Darren hoped she hadn't died in the cottage. Or if she had, that she wasn't haunting it now.

The interior of the house was bright and looked reasonably modern. There was even a conservatory with a beautiful view across the bay to the Isle of Mull.

"What did the clearance guys actually do?" Darren asked, pointing to the furniture that was still in the house. He picked up an old newspaper that was lying on the floor in the living room.

Maggie shrugged. "They only took the really worn items and cleared out the cupboards, so nobody will open a wardrobe and stumble across a dead lady's underwear. They do the big stuff, and we do the rest." She took the old newspaper from Darren's hand and stuffed it into a bin liner.

"Do you do this often?"

"What?"

"Clearing out the house of a dead person. I'd have thought that would be the relatives' job."

Maggie shrugged again. "We get that every now and then. I guess almost half the homes Libby sells belonged to people who died. Apparently there are a fair few heirs who have no use for an old shack at the end of the world.

And some leave the clear-out to us, especially if they live overseas."

She pulled open the drawer of a pretty sideboard with carved wooden doors and looked inside. It was empty, so she pushed it shut again with a slightly disappointed look. "Unfortunately, their lawyers usually drop by first to collect all the valuables."

"So how does Libby get those clients?"

"I'm not sure. Maybe she gets a tip-off. Or someone hands out her leaflets at the funeral parlour. Who knows, maybe she bumps off the old dears herself and leaves her business card in the hall as a farewell." Maggie winked.

She went into the kitchen and opened one of the cupboards. Darren heard her cursing and followed.

"What's up?"

"They forgot to do the kitchen. Look at that!"

She pointed at a stockpile of old jams, spices and tins. There was even an open pack of crumpets that had turned mouldy. Next to the tea and coffee were two tins with the logo of Argyll Herbs and Teas. Apparently Granny Erica wasn't the only one who swore by their healthy herbal teas.

"Just leave it. I'll take care of it," Darren offered generously.

Maggie looked at him in surprise. "Really? That would be great. I hate dirty kitchens."

Darren grinned. "You can do the hoovering instead."

Maggie sighed. "Okay."

"And the window cleaning."

She put her hands on her hips. "Now you're asking too much!"

Darren shrugged and grinned. "It was worth a try. Alright, we'll do the windows together."

After Maggie had disappeared upstairs, Darren grabbed a large bin liner and stuffed the old and expired food in it.

As he was taking the second bag of rubbish outside, a post van stopped in the drive. Andrew Birtwistle stuck his head out the driver's window.

"Sorry, if you've got post for Mrs Attwood, you're a bit too late," Darren deadpanned and put the rubbish down next to the drive.

The postman laughed. "So I heard. No. I just wanted to see how you're getting on."

Darren shrugged. "What for?"

"Let's call it professional curiosity. I wanted to know whether there'll be a new owner soon. In which case I'd have to put the place back on my route."

Darren shook his head. "I don't think you'll have to do that any time soon. We haven't even finished clearing out yet."

"I see." Birtwistle looked around curiously. "Is your gorgeous colleague here as well?"

"Maggie? She's upstairs. Shall I call her?"

The postman waved dismissively. "Nah, no need. I'd have liked to see her though. You've got to admit she's quite a sight."

"Uh-huh." While Birtwistle wasn't wrong, that didn't mean it was ok that Maggie was being ogled by an old geezer like him. Even though he was fit for someone in his fifties, he was more than twice Maggie's age.

Meanwhile, the postman looked up hopefully at the upstairs windows. Does he think she's cleaning naked up there, Darren wondered sourly. With a bit more vigour than necessary, he hurled the bag of rubbish onto the heap piling up next to the drive.

Birtwistle finally managed to tear his gaze away from the house. He briefly looked at Darren and the bin liner, from which half a packet of coffee and a tin of herbal tea were spilling out.

"Alright then. Looks like I won't need to stop here for a while longer. Although of course it's a shame about poor Virginia. Mrs Attwood was such a lovely lady," he said regretfully.

When Darren didn't respond, the postman waved briefly and drove off.

What a bellend, Darren thought as his gaze followed the red post van. His grandmother liked the guy, but Darren realised he agreed with Uncle Greg as far as Birtwistle was concerned.

It took him another half an hour to clear out all the cupboards, the pantry and the fridge. After that, he still had to clean everything.

When Maggie poked her head into the kitchen, he was nearly finished.

"Shall we make ourselves a coffee?" she asked.

"Sure!" He eyed his colleague, who looked striking even in her stained jeans and pinned-up hair. "Did you know Birtwistle was here?"

"Who?"

"The postie. He asked about you by the way."

"Really? What did he want?"

"I don't know. To ogle you, I suppose."

Maggie laughed. "You're not jealous, are you?" she teased him.

Darren snorted derisively. "Of course not. Why should I be jealous of such an old geezer?"

"He's not that old, and his salt and pepper hair makes him look experienced."

"What? Are you telling me you fancy him?"

Maggie grinned. "Only joking. Besides, he doesn't have enough money. I told you I'm looking for a proper rich laird." She winked and pushed past him into the kitchen.

Darren's pulse quickened from the brief touch, but Maggie didn't seem to notice. She looked inside the cupboards, but apart from a few cups and saucers they were all empty.

"Did you throw away all the coffee?" she asked reproachfully.

"Of course." Darren shrugged. Then he realised what his colleague meant. He hung his head. "I didn't think of that. But seriously, do you really want to drink a dead woman's coffee?"

Maggie shrugged. "Why not? It's not like she'll need it anymore." Then she went to the kitchen table, where her bag was. "Looks like we'll have to make do with this." She pulled out a tin from Argyll Herbs and Teas.

Darren's eyes went wide. "Herbal tea?! Are you serious?"

"Back home in Poland we often drink herbal tea. Most of them are quite nice. Let's see what we've got here."

She turned the tin around to read the list of ingredients. That's when Darren caught a glimpse of the label.

"Why did you bring tea for rheumatism? Are you ill?"

Surprised, Maggie turned the tin round. "Oh, you're right. I hadn't even noticed that." Then she went on skimming the ingredients. "Dandelion, rosehip, elderflower—doesn't sound too bad. Shall I make us some?"

Darren eyed her suspiciously. "Why didn't you know what kind of tea you bought?"

"Because I didn't buy it. I found it. Do you know how expensive the teas in that shop are? Old Mrs Attwood won't need it anymore, and you would've just thrown it away. Come on, I'll make us one."

Darren groaned. "I hate herbal tea. How about you get us a proper coffee from Costa? I'll pay."

"As you wish." She put the tin back in her bag and dug out her car keys. "You can get on with the windows while I'm away," she announced with a sweet smile. "The conservatory still needs doing."

CHAPTER 21

When Darren finally got home, his grandmother was already waiting for him.

"How was your date with Katie? Did you have a good time?" Her eyes sparkled.

"What? Yeah, it was quite nice." Darren was too tired to respond to Granny Erica's innuendo. Besides, the busy afternoon in the Attwood house made his date with Katie seem like days ago.

His grandmother was disappointed by his lack of enthusiasm. "Just quite nice? To be honest, I was hoping for more after the effort I put into convincing her that you're not a habitual liar trying to get her into trouble."

Darren sighed. "I am grateful, Granny. Really. It was great with Katie, but can we leave it till tomorrow? I don't feel like talking any more today."

Then suddenly he remembered what Katie had told him. He had nearly forgotten about it after all the work at the Attwood house. "She said there were others!"

"Other what?"

"Katie told me there were more sudden deaths. Similar to Susan Shepherd's. Apparently all who died lived here in the area."

Granny Erica listened up. "Did she mention any names?"

Darren shook his head. "No, data protection."

His grandmother nodded thoughtfully. "But if they lived around here, I should know most of them. What else do you know about them?"

"Not much. Only that there must have been at least three within the last couple of years." He thought of something else. "Did you know a Mrs Attwood?"

"Virginia Attwood? She is one of them?"

Darren shrugged his shoulders. "I don't know. But she died recently and she lived on her own not far from Ganavan. We tidied up her house today, so Libby can start with viewings soon."

Granny Erica thoughtfully tapped her lip. "Unfortunately I didn't know her very well." She gave Darren an impatient look. "What are you waiting for? If we're going to do any serious investigation work tonight, we should at least have a proper drink!"

Darren stared at her in tortured disbelief. "But I'm totally knackered."

"Don't be such a wuss."

He sighed and obediently got the whisky from the cupboard. He put two glasses and a small jug of water on the table. Yet just as he was going to pour the whisky, his grandmother raised a hand.

"Wait. I think I know what we got to do. Put the whisky back, we'll need that."

Bewildered, Darren looked at his grandmother, but she didn't say any more. As he put the bottle back in the cupboard, he glanced towards the dark corner of the room where he could just about make out his grandfather. Darren raised a quizzical eyebrow and nodded towards his grandmother. His grandfather's ghost raised his hands to indicate he was just as baffled. He smiled, although Darren thought there was a hint of pity in his face as well.

He slumped into the hard wooden chair next to his grandmother and poured some water into his empty whisky glass.

"Alright, Granny. What do we need to do?"

Granny Erica grinned. "I can tell you what *you* need to do." She listed a number of things she wanted him to get the next day. But she absolutely refused to tell him what they were for or what she would be doing.

After his grandmother had gone to bed, Darren pondered whether he should pour himself a wee dram after all, but he was so tired that he just made himself a sandwich for dinner before collapsing on the sofa.

The next evening when Darren came home after work and shopping for his grandmother, he heard voices coming from her tiny cottage. Baudrons glared at him from his perch on the garden fence. He seemed to blame Darren for the fact that his cosy home had turned into a madhouse tonight.

Darren opened the door and paused. Granny's friends Janet and Norma were sitting at the dining table, giggling like little girls. At the head of the table sat the postie, Andrew Birtwistle. He was in plain clothes and had a half-full glass of whisky in front of him. There were glasses in front of his grandmother and her friends as well. The bottle of Tobermory, from which Darren and his granny had a couple of drinks a few days ago, stood empty by the sink.

"Excellent. Fresh supplies." Granny Erica beamed up at him.

Obediently, Darren placed a bottle of Glenmorangie on the table before putting the rest of the shopping away in the cupboards and fridge. When he had finished, there was a brief knock on the door and Uncle Greg came in.

He surveyed the gathering without much enthusiasm. When he saw the postman, his face darkened, but he sat down on the last free dining chair without comment.

"What do you want to drink?" Granny Erica asked him.

Greg looked at the whisky glasses on the table. When he got to Birtwistle's, Darren thought the postman looked a little guilty. But you couldn't really tell, as he was smiling pleasantly, and his flushed face might have been caused by the alcohol.

"Have you got any beer?" Greg asked.

Darren nodded and fetched two bottles of Innis & Gunn from the fridge. He gave one to Greg and kept the other for himself. Then he slumped on the sofa.

"Right then, Granny. What's going on here?"

Granny Erica beamed at him. "I've invited our friends so we can tackle your case with our combined knowledge."

Darren nearly choked on his beer. "My what?"

His grandmother thrust her chin forward defiantly. "Your case. It's not looking like you'll be able to crack it on your own, so I got help. It was one thing when it was only about poor Sue Shepherd, but what you told me yesterday suggests there's a serial killer on the loose here in Ganavan. That means we all have to rack our brains now!"

Darren put his beer on the floor and bent towards his grandmother. "I never said anything like that!" he hissed, glancing distrustfully at Andrew Birtwistle and his grandmother's friends. "If anyone finds out what you've done with Katie's confidential information, you'll get her in big trouble!"

Granny Erica patted his hand reassuringly. "Don't fret. None of us will tell anyone. We're among friends here!"

"What did you just say about a serial killer, Erica?" Janet interrupted. "Is that true? Or are you just trying to scare us again? And what do the police have to say about it?"

Norma also stared at her wide-eyed.

Erica turned towards the table and looked at everyone in turn. "Right then. The reason I invited you all here tonight is that we need your help. It's true, it looks like there's a serial killer on the loose in Ganavan. The police don't know anything about it, because the victims are all old folk like us, and the doctors at the hospital didn't flag their deaths as suspicious. However, Darren and I are fairly certain that they didn't all die of natural causes."

Now she really had the attention of her guests.

Greg threw Darren a quizzical look. Darren subtly shrugged his shoulders and turned his eyes towards the ceiling, as if pleading for help. Greg shook his head almost imperceptibly and hid a smirk by taking a sip of his beer.

"What makes you think that?" Norma asked.

Granny Erica looked at Darren. Panicked, he thought about what he should say, but before he could open his mouth, his grandmother went on.

"To be honest, so far it's more of a gut feeling. The first victim we learned about was poor Sue Shepherd from Pennyfuir. She was perfectly healthy until one day she dropped dead."

Darren's eyes widened in surprise. "But that's not—" he started. Granny Erica ignored him.

"Then a couple of weeks ago Mrs Attwood died," she continued unperturbed. "And then we, well, me, realised that rather a lot of the elderly in Ganavan and nearby have died recently. Including quite a few I wouldn't have expected to. That can't all be natural."

"So what do you think is happening?" the postman asked. "I mean, why would anyone want to kill those old people?"

Granny Erica raised her hands. "We don't know. Not yet anyway. That's another reason we wanted your help."

Birtwistle nodded thoughtfully.

"Are you absolutely sure Mrs Attwood and Sue Shepherd were murdered?" Greg asked.

Granny Erica hesitated. "No," she admitted. "If it was that clear-cut, we would have got the police involved by now."

"So, what exactly do you expect us to do?"

That was something Darren was curious to hear as well.

"Very simple. We've all lived in Ganavan for a long time and should know most of the victims. First, I want you to think about everyone who died within the last two or three years. Then we pick out those whose deaths were unexpected or very sudden. And finally, we try to find out what they have in common. That way, we ought to be able to get to the bottom of the matter."

"So what's he doing here?" Greg nodded towards Birtwistle.

Granny Erica looked at him. "I'm sure Andrew could help us. His job takes him around the whole area and he knows lots of people."

"Of course I'll help you, Erica!" Birtwistle smiled amiably.

Greg grumbled.

"And you want to do all that tonight?" Janet asked with astonishment. "Even detectives in murder mysteries usually get several days."

"Oh, Janet. Do you have to be such a defeatist all the time? Just imagine we're in a John Rebus episode. He solves his cases in less than two hours, and we're much better than him, aren't we? Right, let's get started."

Silence descended upon the table while everyone went through their friends and acquaintances who had passed away in recent years.

Norma was the first to come up with a name. "Mrs Myles. The one with the old house down by Ganavan Sands. She died about a year ago."

Uncle Greg frowned. "Didn't she fall off a ladder?"

"So what? Erica wanted unexpected and sudden deaths. Who says she wasn't pushed?"

Granny Erica nodded. "You're right. Put Mrs Myles on our list, Darren." That settled the matter.

Over the next hour, they came up with fourteen more deaths in Ganavan and the surrounding area within the last two years. They were able to rule out about half of them due to known illnesses or because it seemed impossible that someone could have deliberately staged such a death.

"What about Peter Knops?" Janet asked.

"I don't think we need to put him on the list. He fell off the roof during a storm last autumn."

Darren frowned. "What was he doing up there in a storm?"

Granny Erica shrugged. "Apparently he wanted to fix some problem with his satellite dish."

"But why then?"

"He was a passionate Celtic fan, and there was going to be a match that night. However, I don't think he would have climbed onto the roof if he had been entirely sober."

Janet shook her head. "His wife used to say that football would be his death eventually, and so it was."

"So I don't put him down?" Darren made sure.

His grandmother shook her head.

In the end, they had seven names left. If they had considered Granny Erica's theory about a serial killer a figment of her overactive imagination to start with, things looked different now. Seven elderly people dying unexpectedly in such a small neighbourhood couldn't be coincidence. There was no denying it, something sinister was happening in Ganavan, and a serial killer targeting the elderly seemed the most likely explanation.

"How are we going to find out what they had in common?" Janet asked nervously. She had gone very pale when Erica had read out the final list.

"I'm more interested in how we can avoid being added to the list ourselves," Norma mumbled. She poured herself another whisky to calm her nerves.

Greg stood up abruptly. "Well, I need a break." He grabbed his jacket and went outside.

Darren followed him. Surprised, he watched as Greg pulled a packet of tobacco out of his pocket and rolled himself a cigarette. "When did you start smoking?"

Greg looked up. "Oh, it's you, Chubby Cheeks." Then he concentrated on his hands again. Only when he had finished and had taken a long drag, he replied. "I actually quit smoking years ago, but sometimes I still feel the urge."

He looked Darren in the eyes. "Can you please tell me what's going on in there? Your story about Sue Shepherd and the ghost of old Tony was outlandish enough. But where did your grandmother suddenly get this crazy idea about a serial killer?"

Darren sighed. "Katie discovered that there were other cases similar to Sue's. Elderly people who had previously been healthy suddenly dying without obvious cause."

"Katie?"

"Katie Beales. She's a nurse at the hospital in Oban."

"The one at the concert, with the curly hair?"

Darren nodded.

Greg blew smoke into the cold night air. "But why does Erica suddenly fancy herself as Miss Marple?"

"I don't know. I think to begin with she just thought it an interesting story. She was intrigued when I told her about Tony and his wife. But if there really is something to it…"

"…she could be in danger too," Greg finished Darren's sentence.

Darren nodded, then shrugged his shoulders. "Maybe. I don't know."

Greg looked at him thoughtfully. "I think it might be something to do with the houses. In that case your grandmother would only be in danger if the murderer thinks she could harm him."

"Which houses? Their homes?" Darren frowned confused.

"Aye. It's quite simple. I noticed that none of the people on the list had relatives nearby. Some of them didn't have anyone at all. The others live in America or London or wherever. So I suppose most of their homes where sold as quickly as possible. Maybe there's some sort of property scam going on here."

Darren couldn't suppress a smirk. "Are you turning into a conspiracist now?"

Greg grinned wryly. "Quite possibly. But if I'm right, at least Erica should be safe, because she's got you."

Darren nodded. "On the other hand, I've only been here for a couple of weeks. Before, someone could easily have thought she was alone. After all, my father and his new wife have been living in Florida for ages. He hasn't been to Ganavan in years."

Greg scratched his chin thoughtfully. "Aye, you're right there. In any case, she shouldn't boast about knowing what's behind these deaths. Not in front of her friends, and certainly not in front of that Birtwistle. Who knows who else will get to hear about it."

Darren felt the same. "So, what do we do now?"

"*We* won't do anything, because I'm going home now. But *you* should find out more about the victims' properties tomorrow. And try to stop your grandmother from playing Miss Marple."

"Alright."

Greg nodded. "Good lad."

He stubbed out his cigarette in a flowerpot and put it in his pocket. Then he raised a hand in goodbye and trudged off into the night. Darren was left with the near impossible task of reining in his grandmother.

Fortunately, it turned out to be easier than expected. Janet and Norma were more than a little tipsy, and quite ready to postpone further investigations to another day. As Darren had only had the one beer, he offered to drive them home, which they gladly accepted.

Janet announced she would avoid walking around Ganavan alone at night for the time being, while Norma decided that such caution was unnecessary. After all, they weren't looking for a thug, but for a stealthy villain who bumped off his victims without anyone noticing, probably using poison. That thought didn't seem to cheer up Janet though.

Andrew Birtwistle was also ready to postpone the murder hunt to another day. After all, he had to start his round again early the next morning. So, barely half an hour after Greg had gone home, their party had dispersed.

"Wasn't this a great idea?" Granny Erica beamed at Darren when he returned. "It would have taken us ages to come up with all those names on our own."

Darren agreed cautiously and slumped down at the table, exhausted.

"Uncle Greg thinks we shouldn't tell everyone that we're looking for a murderer."

"Like I was blabbing about it to the whole village," his grandmother huffed, "when I only mentioned it to our friends."

"Still, it won't hurt to be discreet."

He wondered whether he should tell his grandmother about Greg's hunch about the victims' homes, but decided against it. Uncle Greg was right, Granny Erica seemed to enjoy her role as an amateur sleuth a little too much. Besides, the less anyone knew about his suspicions, the better. For now anyway.

Later, when he was lying on the sofa, another thought occurred to Darren. While their houses might be something all victims had in common, there was more that connected them. They all had lived alone, and they would have known their murderer. He or she must have found a way to administer the poison without arousing suspicion. Darren imagined how some old lady invited her murderer into her home. Maybe because the person was helping them with something.

This meant they should be looking for someone who knew lots of people in Ganavan and whom they trusted. Someone like Marcy from the Women's Institute, whom he still hadn't met. Or someone like Greg, who was known for his readiness to help and his DIY skills.

The idea that Greg might be their serial killer was, of course, completely absurd. After all, Darren had known him since childhood. Nevertheless, a gnawing doubt remained as Darren tried to fall asleep.

CHAPTER 22

The next morning, Darren was more refreshed than his grandmother for once. He had already made coffee when she came hobbling out of her bedroom with her hair still dishevelled.

"Headache?" he asked sympathetically, hiding his smirk behind his mug.

Granny Erica held her head and groaned. "Could you make me a headache tea, please? Or, if there isn't any of that left, I'll have the rheumatism tea instead."

Darren raised an eyebrow. "I didn't know you suffered from rheumatism?"

She waved her hand defensively. "Of course not. It was a gift, but it helps with a sore head, so I kept it."

Darren wondered just how often his grandmother needed a hangover cure. But as he didn't think she was in the mood for his teasing right now, he swallowed his remark. Instead, he rummaged through the cupboard until he found the packet of tea she wanted. It was from Argyll Herbs and Teas, of course.

"They're doing good business," Darren remarked while shaking what remained of the headache tea into a tea pot before pouring boiling water over it.

"No wonder, their teas are tasty and work better than most pills. Besides, the tins make great presents."

Darren picked up a tin decorated with thistles and other flowers, which had been hidden behind the headache tea. It really was quite pretty.

"But who'd give you rheumatism tea as a present?"

Granny Erica grimaced. "Andrew gave it to me after I took him along for an Antiques rehearsal. But you're right, I'd have preferred a box of chocolates."

Darren grinned. "Because it wouldn't have made you feel like quite such an old bag?"

"What nonsense!" she protested, but Darren saw she was blushing.

Still grinning, he poured her a cup of headache tea.

He spent the rest of the morning doing research on his laptop. Greg had been right. Most of the homes of the deceased had been sold through local estate agents. Only one seemed to have gone to a nephew or cousin who probably had been looking for a new place anyway.

Darren was unnerved by the fact that the estate agent in almost all the cases had been Libby Whatmough, his boss.

It could be coincidence of course. After all, Maggie had told him that lots of the homes she sold were on behalf of the heirs. That still left the question, how did Libby get those clients?

On further investigation he found that she had sold many of the homes of the non-suspicious cases as well. Was it all just coincidence after all?

Shortly before lunchtime, he rang Katie Beales. They had agreed to meet in Oban in the afternoon, but Libby had called on short notice because she wanted one of her properties prepared for a viewing. Maybe that would be a good opportunity to sound her out, Darren thought.

Katie was disappointed when he cancelled their date, but it couldn't be helped.

When he told her of the progress he had made and read out the list of names that Granny Erica and her friends had compiled the previous evening, the line went quiet.

"Katie? Are you still there?" Darren asked after he hadn't heard anything for nearly a minute.

Eventually he heard a rustling. "Katie? Is that you?"

"What? Yes, sorry. I was just looking for my own list. Could you read out the names again please?"

Darren slowly repeated each of the seven names.

He could hear Katie's breath quickening. "Are you okay?"

"Yes. Three of the names are on my list as well, and I've noted down the others so I can check them."

"Do you also think there's a serial killer on the loose?"

"I wish I knew," Katie said. "But you have to admit it's worrying."

Darren pondered. "Have you got any way to find out what might have caused their symptoms?"

"I'll try. But if they were poisoned, it must have been something slow-acting. They must have taken it without realising."

"What makes you say that?"

"According to the files, they all called 999 themselves. I don't think any of them claimed they had been poisoned. Otherwise there would have been an investigation long ago."

"That makes sense. But what was it? And how were they made to take it?"

"I'll try to find out," Katie promised. "Or at least figure out how it might have been done."

Then they arranged to meet in the evening.

The house Libby wanted to have prepared was in a small village called Lochdon on the Isle of Mull. When he had been talking to her, Darren doubted he would be able to get a ferry ticket to Mull that day, but she had already booked one for him.

"Didn't you say you had local staff for your island properties?" he had asked her. Darren didn't fancy spending all afternoon on the island and not getting back until late in the evening, if at all.

"Mrs McKay called in sick, and I have no one else on such short notice," Libby had explained. "Don't make a fuss. The ferry doesn't even take an hour."

He had no choice but to get to the ferry terminal in Oban on time. After his call with Katie, he said goodbye to his grandma and sped down the coastal road in the little Corsa.

By the time he reached the terminal, most of the other cars had already rolled up the loading ramp into the belly of the big ferry. The lane for last-minute bookings was just being opened, but as he already had a ticket, they waved him past to drive straight on board.

Soon after, all the vehicles were loaded and the ferry's doors were closed, ready for the short crossing to Mull. Darren went upstairs with the other passengers, to watch the boat slowly leaving Oban behind.

On the left, they passed the small harbour of Kerrera and the obelisk of Hutcheson's Monument. Shortly after, the overgrown ruin of Dunollie Castle and tiny Maiden Island came into view on the right. Finally, the ferry set course towards the Isle of Mull.

It had been years since Darren had last been to Mull, even though it was only a short distance from Oban. The crossing past Lismore Lighthouse and Duart Castle must be among Caledonian MacBrayne's more spectacular ferry routes.

Maybe he could take Katie on a day trip there some time. They could drive over to Tobermory or go hiking somewhere, although of course not before this business about the Ganavan serial killer was resolved.

The thought of someone targeting the elderly homeowners of Ganavan made Darren shudder. Even though he failed to imagine Libby as a killer, there seemed to be a connection. It was simply too much of a coincidence that most of the suspected victims' homes had been sold by her.

Meanwhile, the ferry had passed Duart Castle, rising grey and forbidding on a rock overlooking the Sound of Mull. As the boat was turning towards the pier in Craignure, the passengers were asked to return to their vehicles. Soon after, Darren and the other passengers disembarked.

The drive to Lochdon barely took five minutes. The more difficult part was finding the right house. Unlike the stately villas Libby was selling around Oban, there were only bungalows and tiny stone houses here. Darren slowly drove along the shore of Loch Don until he spotted Libby's 'For Sale' sign. He found the house keys under a rock next to the door, as she had told him.

The tiny crofter cottage was whitewashed and had a chimney at each gable end. There couldn't be more than one bedroom, as it looked like the same layout as his grandmother's home. It was far too small for a family, even though a hundred years ago up to three generations would have dwelt under that one roof. But who would be happy with such a small place these days? For buyers there was really only one solution—Mull was popular with tourists, so maybe someone would want to turn it into a holiday home.

Fortunately, there wasn't much that needed to be done in the house and its small front garden. After a bit of an airing and sweeping out the dust and cobwebs of last winter, the property would be ready for tomorrow's viewing. It was going to take Darren longer to travel here and back than it would to clean and prepare the place. At least Libby would have to pay him for his travel time.

Darren was pleased he would be able to catch the earlier ferry, but just as he was about to get in his car, Libby drew up in her silver BMW X5.

"How are you getting on?" she asked.

The estate agent cast a critical eye over the front garden with its sparse daffodil beds. Apart from a bit of lawn, the daffodils and a lonely leafless bush, the garden didn't offer much cheer. To the left were a space for the bins and a small stack of firewood.

"At least it's not as overgrown as that horrible thicket around Rose Cottage," she sighed. "Although the bins would be better behind the house."

She asked Darren for the keys, unlocked the front door, and gestured for him to join her. He obediently trudged after her. The interior was simple and noticeably more modern than the outside of the cottage suggested. There wasn't much furniture, but the wooden floor was clean. Libby soon declared herself satisfied apart from a few minor details. "Alright, this should be fine for tomorrow."

Darren nodded, but instead of leaving, he hesitated. He didn't want to pass up the opportunity to talk to Libby alone.

"What's up?"

The estate agent seemed impatient. Darren wondered whether this was the right time to confront her about the suspicious deaths in Ganavan, but at least she would find it difficult to evade his questions here. This might be his best chance to find out if his boss was a devious poisoner. The question was how? She was hardly going to admit to poisoning Sue Shepherd.

"I wanted to ask you something. About the homes you sell," he began.

Libby raised an eyebrow. "Have you found one you like?"

"No. It's more about how you know that a house will be for sale."

Libby looked at him appraisingly. "You probably want to earn a little extra too. It's true, I'm happy to pay a small bonus for a good tip-off. Did Maggie tell you about it?"

Darren hesitated, then shook his head. Was there a reason why his colleague hadn't mentioned it? Maybe she just didn't want him to beat her to a tip. There could be more to it though. Maggie had made no secret about being in Scotland to make money, and she had had no qualms about bagging the tea at the Attwood house. If she happened to find valuables while clearing out a home, Darren wouldn't rely on her handing them over to their boss.

"Let's get to the point then. What's this about?" Libby was getting impatient now.

Darren focussed on her eyes. "Did you know that most of your homes are from people who died recently?" he blurted out. He would find out later whether Maggie had anything to do with it.

He watched Libby's expression closely but could spot neither surprise nor guilt.

"Yes, of course. So? Those are the ones that most frequently come onto the market."

"But did you also know that a suspicious number of homeowners in the Ganavan area died in the last couple of years? Died unexpectedly, I should say. And you sold almost all their properties."

This time the estate agent blinked in surprise, but he couldn't tell whether she was surprised by the deaths or by Darren's knowledge of them.

"What are you implying?"

Darren hesitated.

"If the heirs want to get rid of the homes, why shouldn't I sell them? I'm an estate agent after all." Libby crossed her arms in front of her chest and glared at him defiantly. "The property business is a tough one. I didn't become so successful by being squeamish."

Darren frowned. Was that a confession? Surely not. He needed more than that. "That's exactly what I mean. You're not squeamish when it comes to acquiring new houses."

"Excuse me? It's not my fault that people die."

He didn't reply.

Libby's eyes narrowed. "Is that what you think of me? That I give them a push? That I'd kill someone for the lousy commission I might get from selling their home?" Her eyes sparkled with indignation.

Darren hesitated. How much commission did estate agents actually get? Quite a lot, he assumed. On the other hand, Libby had properties like the castle hotel in her portfolio. That probably sold for several million, with a five-figure commission coming her way. Why would she kill someone for the relative peanuts she'd get from Rose Cottage? It didn't make sense.

"No," he admitted eventually. "I don't think you killed anyone, but there still must be some connection. I don't believe that it's all just coincidence," he added helplessly.

"I'm glad you don't think I'm a murderer," she said sarcastically. "But why don't you start at the beginning? What isn't a coincidence?"

"Sue Shepherd and Mrs Attwood and some others. They all died rather suddenly and now you're selling their homes."

Libby's eyes flashed angrily. "I have no idea what you're implying, but I've had enough. I hope for your sake that you haven't spread your false accusations anywhere, because I can assure you that I'll sue for slander if you do. Now give me those keys and get out!"

Darren stared at her incredulously. True, he had just accused her of murder, but he had already admitted that he had been wrong. Why didn't she see the link between the deaths and her estate agency? There had to be a connection.

"GET OUT!"

Darren winced. Without another word, he pressed the keys into her hand, got in the car and fled.

As he waited in line for the ferry in Craignure, he cursed silently. His heart was still pounding after what had just happened. But what was he going to do now?

Unless she was an incredibly good actress, Libby was no killer. She might have a motive, but a murder—never mind a whole series of murders—was a very high risk for a successful businesswoman like her. She couldn't expect them to go unnoticed in the long run. Besides, Darren wasn't even certain that she had known the victims personally.

Yet something was going on here. He could feel it. Did Libby know more than she was letting on? Maybe she had an inkling who might be behind it.

Darren wondered if it could be Maggie. She had kept Libby's offer to reward tip-offs from him, and she wanted money. Then again, she had told him she had only been working for Libby for three years. So how would she have known all those people who had died in Ganavan in the last couple of years?

He tried to focus on everything he knew about the killer. Didn't he have a few ideas shortly before he fell asleep last night? But no matter how much he turned things over in his mind, he could not make heads nor tails of the matter. He urgently needed to talk to someone about it.

When he was on the ferry, he sent Katie a message, asking her to meet him in Oban if she was free. He was lucky—her shift was over and she agreed to meet him at the ferry pier.

Although the weather was mild, neither of them fancied going for a walk. So they went to the Corryvreckan, a big and somewhat impersonal chain pub by the harbour. Darren got drinks from the bar, then Katie asked about his day on Mull.

He sighed and recounted the conversation with his boss.

She shook her head and laughed when he told her about Libby's reaction. "Did you seriously think she'd confess a murder just like that?"

"No. But I was hoping she might let something slip if I surprise her." He grinned, half apologetic, half resigned. "How would you have tackled the issue?"

"Certainly not charging in head-on like that. With a bit more discretion."

Darren shrugged. "You do the next serial killer," he offered generously. "But what do we do now? Have you found out anything about Susan's symptoms?"

Katie sighed. "Not as much as I'd have liked. I think it must have been something natural."

"Why?"

"Dangerous drugs are much harder to get hold of than plants. Besides, drugs are usually too bitter to mix into anything without being noticed. That's a precaution by the manufacturers to prevent accidental overdoses."

"I see. What could it have been then?"

"I asked a colleague and she told me there are several possibilities. Lily of the valley would be one."

"Are they in blossom already?"

"Doesn't matter. Any part of the plant will do. The berries are the most poisonous. Someone could have mixed dried, ground berries into Sue Shepherd's porridge oats."

Darren nodded thoughtfully. "That would mean the person needed access to her kitchen. I'm afraid that doesn't help us much though."

"But we know a lot more now than we did when we started."

"True enough," Darren agreed, even though most was still guesswork.

Darren soon said goodnight. He would have liked to stay but he wanted to check on his grandmother. Katie had to leave too.

"I've got the early shift tomorrow," she apologised.

Darren nodded. He was glad that he could organise his own working hours, at least on the rare days when Grandma Erica didn't do it for him.

CHAPTER 23

It was well after dark when Darren got back to Ganavan. The streets were deserted and the lights in his grandmother's home were off. After parking the car, he pulled out the key that Granny Erica had given him, but when he got to the door, he found it unlocked.

Perplexed, Darren entered the living room. Baudrons came to greet him, rubbing against his legs and mewing. His food bowl was empty. An open packet of tea sat on the sideboard.

Darren fetched the cat food. He couldn't remember his grandmother ever forgetting to feed her fat cat. Then he noticed that her jacket, which usually hung by the door, was gone. He tried to remember if she had mentioned she was going out. How though, with that cast?

Then he recalled it was band practice today. The Ganavan Antiques wanted to meet at the school, and his grandmother had probably been picked up by one of the band members. That also explained the tea and the unlocked door. She was probably running a bit late and had left in a hurry.

He took a mug from the cupboard, put the kettle on, and took a tea bag from the open packet. When he put the tea back in the cupboard, he noticed that the tin of rheumatism tea he had seen that morning was gone. He smiled. Granny Erica had probably given it away because he had called her an old bag.

Suddenly something occurred to him. He rang Katie.

"That poisonous herb you mentioned, could it be added to tea?"

Katie thought about that. "I suppose, but I don't know if you'd taste it."

"What if I used herbal tea? Rheumatism tea, for example?"

"That might work. What made you think of that?"

"It was just an idea. Thank you!" Darren hung up.

He looked down at Baudrons, who had finished his dinner and was begging to be stroked. Darren sat on the sofa and patted the seat to prompt the cat to join him. Baudrons didn't need much invitation. He climbed onto Darren's knees and purred appreciatively when Darren petted him.

It was unusually quiet in the house without his grandmother. Even the purring cat didn't change that. Darren wondered why the silence seemed so strange, until he realised that the fire had gone out. His grandmother had obviously been gone for some time. She would be miffed if she came back to find that he hadn't even lit the oven.

Sighing, he busied himself with getting the fire going again. Once it was burning and started to fill the room with warmth, it occurred to Darren that his grandmother might be hungry when she got home from band practice. Maybe he could convince her to bring fish and chips for them both.

He dialled her number, glad she had finally got herself a mobile phone. To his surprise, the old-fashioned ringtone she had chosen sounded somewhere nearby. After a bit of searching, he found her phone behind the sofa. Why hadn't he noticed that before? Granny Erica's handbag was lying next to the sofa. The case with the bagpipes had been carelessly chucked on the floor. This wasn't like her at all. And why were her bagpipes here anyway? Surely she would have taken them with her to band practice. Had something happened? Obviously she had been in a rush.

He scrolled through the contact list on his phone until he found Greg's number.

"Is Granny Erica with you?" he asked without preamble.

It took a moment for Greg to respond. "No. Why would she?"

"She's disappeared."

"How do you mean? Have you mislaid her? Has she vanished into thin air?"

"No idea, but she's not at home."

Greg didn't seem overly perturbed. "So? She's probably still at band practice." Even though he wasn't a regular member of the Antiques, he obviously knew when they were rehearsing.

"Her bagpipes are here though, and her phone too."

"Hmm," Greg considered. "Maybe she's with Janet or Norma."

"I'll call them," Darren said, although he was starting to worry. Why would Granny Erica visit her friends at their homes with her foot in a cast? It was much easier to invite them here.

After some searching, he found their phone numbers on a piece of paper in her bedside table. As he held it, he cursed himself. Why hadn't he thought of calling them on his grandmother's mobile? She must have saved them there.

"Aunt Norma? Is Granny Erica with you?"

"No, but it's good I get to talk to you. Libby called me. She said you accused her of criminal activity. How could you, Darren? After I vouched for you."

He had almost forgotten about Libby. "I'm sorry. I'll apologise to her tomorrow, but I thought I was on to something."

"What are you talking about?"

"About the deaths in Ganavan. Our serial killer. All the victims lived on their own. And Libby later sold their homes. All their homes. There must be a connection."

"What would that be? You don't believe my niece killed them, do you?"

"No, but I think somebody benefited from killing those people. Maybe indirectly. Libby might have paid someone."

"To murder our neighbours? What an absurd idea."

"That's not what I meant. But she does pay for tip-offs about properties that might come on the market soon. Empty houses, deaths, divorces, that sort of thing. She told me so herself. Anyway, that's completely beside the point just now. Granny's gone."

"Gone where? What are you talking about?"

"I don't know where she is. She's not at home, but she didn't take her phone."

"Och, laddie. No need to worry. Your grandmother is an adult. She's probably at Janet's."

"But how? Do you think she hobbled all the way across the village with her cast and crutch?"

"I wouldn't put it past her. She was just telling me how much she missed being able to go for a proper walk. She even threatened to hit her doctor over the head with her crutch if he didn't take the cast off soon." Norma laughed. "Although more likely Janet just picked her up in the car. They'll be sitting at her place, chatting away."

"Could be." Darren had his doubts. Janet had told him she didn't like driving at night anymore. Besides, it would have been more convenient to just stay here instead of driving back and forth. So why bother?

"Don't forget to call Libby!" Norma reminded him.

"I won't." He hung up.

He looked around thoughtfully. On impulse, he switched off all the lights apart from one reading lamp.

"Grandpa Alan? Are you there?" he asked into the empty room. He scanned the darkness but didn't see anyone. "Grandpa?"

Still no reply. Suddenly, somebody was banging on the door. The abrupt noise made Darren jump. Before he could get to the door, Greg came in. He was wearing a weatherproof jacket and walking boots and was holding a torch.

"Has she turned up yet?" he asked.

"No."

Greg frowned worriedly. "That's not like her at all. Any ideas?"

Darren shook his head. "Unless she's with Aunt Janet?"

"I called Pete. He said band practice ended half an hour ago. Miss Lindsay needed the room for a parents' meeting tonight, so they finished early. He dropped Erica off here before driving to the pub, so she can't be far. Have you looked in the garden yet?"

"No. What would she be doing there? It's pitch black outside."

"I don't know. Maybe she wanted to get a few herbs for cooking and fell."

"Don't you think she'd have shouted when she heard me arriving in the car?"

Nevertheless, they went and searched the overgrown garden behind the cottage. Yet without success. There was no trace of Granny Erica. Darren noticed that the gate leading to the path to the beach hung open, but it had probably been like that for days.

Darren's phone rang. It was Libby. He rejected the call. Immediately, the phone rang again. Libby again.

Sighing, he pressed the phone to his ear. "I'm sorry, Libby. I didn't mean to insult you." He rattled off his apology without much conviction. "Can we talk tomorrow? I'm really busy just now."

"Suit yourself. But I thought you'd be interested that I might know who's done it."

"Done what?"

"The deaths you blamed on me today. I've just been talking to my aunt Norma, and she also mentioned old folk dying unexpectedly in Ganavan in the past year. She's concerned."

Darren waited, but she didn't say anything more. "So?" he asked impatiently.

Libby hesitated. She sounded defensive when she said, "You must realise I couldn't possibly have known something like that would happen. Your story really sounded like some crazy conspiracy theory."

"Libby!"

"Alright. I believe Birtwistle could have something to do with it."

"The postie?"

"Yes."

"Why him?"

Out of the corner of his eye, Darren saw Greg pulling out his phone. He turned away to concentrate on Libby.

"I thought about my sources in the area and Birtwistle is certainly the most effective. He gets a percentage of my commission if I sell a property he found for me. As a postman he's often the first to hear what's going on in the neighbourhood. That includes empty houses and homes that might come up for sale. But who'd expect him to actively help things along?!"

"Are you sure that's what he does?"

"No, of course not. But there's no one else I can think of. He's the only one north of Oban who gives me tip-offs fairly regularly. And in the last few months he's become increasingly pushy."

"I see. Have you told the police yet?"

"No, of course not. After all, it's only conjecture. I might be wrong. Let's hope I am. Still, I'll talk to Birtwistle tomorrow."

"Hmm."

Greg pointed at Darren's phone and gestured. He was getting impatient. Darren nodded.

"Sorry, Libby, but I have to rush. My grandmother's disappeared. Can we talk about Birtwistle tomorrow?"

"Wait!"

Darren groaned. "What is it?"

"There's more. The reason I called tonight in the first place. A few weeks ago Birtwistle told me that he'd soon have a lovely old croft house for me. Then, a couple days ago, he said that maybe it wouldn't come on the market after all, because a grandson had turned up. That made me think of your grandmother. I wondered if he'd been after her."

"You think he's abducted my grandmother? That's why she's disappeared?"

Libby went quiet for a moment. "No, you're right, that does seem rather absurd. Still, I thought you should know."

"Right, thanks. I'll keep it in mind. Bye for now." He hung up.

He looked at Uncle Greg, who raised a quizzical eyebrow. Darren quickly told him what he had learnt from the estate agent.

Greg frowned. "I always suspected Birtwistle was a wrong 'un," he growled. Then he remembered why he was there. He held up his phone. "I rang Janet while you were talking to Libby. Erica isn't there either."

"Right, so what do we do now? Call the police?"

"No. They wouldn't do anything yet anyway. It's not like she's got dementia, so there's no obvious danger."

"But what else can we do?"

"I don't know." Greg shook his head in frustration. "Show me where you found her things. Maybe that will give us a clue as to where she went."

"Over there." Darren pointed next to the sofa. Then he sank onto a kitchen chair, rested his elbows on the table and ran his hands through his hair. "I just can't imagine where she could have gone. Especially with her bad foot. It's getting better, but she's still got the cast."

The old man grunted in agreement, while rifling through Granny Erica's belongings. "Is her jacket there? Could you have a look?" he asked after a minute.

Darren glanced at the hooks by the front door. "Her jacket's gone." He looked over to Greg. "Do you think she just headed out briefly? I noticed earlier that a tin with rheumatism tea is gone. Maybe she's visiting a neighbour who needs it."

Greg shook his head though. "Who'd that be? Anyone afflicted by rheumatism usually swears by painkillers. And if not, they'd hardly call your grandmother. It's not like she's a healer or something."

Darren nodded pensively, then he turned pale. "The tea! She got it from Birtwistle. And Katie thinks Sue Shepherd might have been poisoned with some kind of herb. Maybe poisonous berries that someone put into a meal or tea. Do you think Granny Erica made herself some tea and poisoned herself? Maybe she's already in hospital!"

Greg snorted. "If an ambulance had come through the village with blues and twos, we'd know about it. Besides, doesn't your girlfriend work at the hospital? Wouldn't she have called you if your grandmother had been brought in?"

Darren nodded. "Yes, I suppose she would have. She'd only just come off duty."

"Then let's get going." Greg grabbed Granny Erica's car key, which was lying on the table, and made for the door.

"Where to?" Darren asked in confusion.

"Where do you think? To Birtwistle's. If Erica is in danger, it's from him."

Darren couldn't argue with that.

CHAPTER 24

Andrew Birtwistle was annoyed. First, Erica's grandson had turned up out of the blue after he had neglected her for months, if not years. Then he started poking his nose into things that were none of his business. And now Libby was griping as well.

He had been working with her for three years. It was she who had asked him to hand out her business cards and leaflets whenever he thought a home might come up for sale. Yet even though she profited much more from their cooperation than he did, she had recently become increasingly dismissive and preferred not to be seen in public with him at all.

Yes, he had helped matters along at a few properties, so they had come on the market a bit sooner than strictly necessary. But Libby didn't know about that. And even if she did, why would she care? The old biddies had been on their last legs anyway. He had done them and the chronically overstretched National Health Service a favour. Besides, nobody could prove anything. He wasn't around when they took the poison, and no one had ever suspected anything. Until now.

It was unfortunate that Mrs Bagshaw's nosy grandson had become suspicious about Sue Shepherd's death. How he got that idea was a complete mystery. He had never even met her. The fact that the wee toerag then realised that there had been other deaths was more than a little annoying.

Nevertheless, Birtwistle was in no real danger so far. All he had to do was keep his head down and avoid attracting attention until the storm had passed. Then he would sort out Libby. Surely she didn't think that she could just kick him out after all the business he had sent her way over the last few years.

Back to his current problem though. It was fortunate that the old Bagshaw had invited him to her conspiratorial gathering. How amused he had been that she had asked him, of all people, to help find the murderer. The precision with which the old birds had identified his victims had been appalling though. Luckily all evidence had been destroyed long ago. All except for one tin of tea.

It had been months since he had handed out his little Christmas presents. Harmless tea for the ladies who had their families nearby. But the lonely old widows got his special mix, to which he had added some dried berries of lily of the valley. It was entirely inconspicuous. Ironically, the poisonous berries actually came from gardens of their victims. How proud they had been of their homes and flower beds. And how grateful when he dropped in once or twice a week for a cuppa and a wee chat.

Just like Erica with her bagpipes. If he had known she would leave the tea untouched in the cupboard for months, he wouldn't have bothered giving her one of his special tins. But with her son living in the States for many years, and her grandson visiting rarely, the chances were good that the son or grandson would simply sell her home if she'd kicked the bucket. A traditional croft house like hers would fetch at least two hundred thousand pounds these days, two thousand of which would have made their way into his account. That's what he had agreed with Libby: he would get a quarter of her commission once the house was sold.

Very well. For the time being there wouldn't be any more income from that source. And unless he was very careful, possibly never again.

Luckily, Birtwistle knew that the Ganavan Antiques had their band practice tonight. Erica would be there with the other oldies, so it shouldn't be a problem to sneak into her home, find the tin with the poisoned tea and dispose of that last piece of evidence.

He parked his car a little distance from his destination in the drive of an unoccupied holiday home. Of course he had come in his private car, which hardly anyone in Ganavan would recognise. Most people only knew him as the driver of the red post van.

Birtwistle went through the garden to the back door of the cottage, knowing that Erica usually left it unlocked. He didn't switch on the light, as it was too visible from the street. He would find his way round anyhow. Sharing a cuppa with the old crones week after week was paying off now.

He quickly crossed the room and fumbled in the kitchen cupboard for the fancy tin from Argyll Herbs and Teas. Nobody could accuse him of being stingy with his gifts. There it was. Contented, he put the tin in his pocket.

Suddenly he felt something rubbing against his calf, followed by loud purring.

"Baudrons! You gave me a fright!"

He bent down to scratch the cat behind his ears. The purring intensified. When he stopped, Baudrons miaowed in protest. Birtwistle obediently scratched his head some more.

"Now I've really got to go," he whispered to the cat. At that moment, man and cat froze, blinded by the ceiling light coming on.

"Andrew, what are you doing here?" Granny Erica asked in surprise.

Birtwistle straightened up. He cursed himself for being so distracted by the cat that he hadn't heard the car that must have dropped her off. Nevertheless, he beamed at the old biddy as if he was overjoyed to see her.

"I… just wanted to check that everything was okay. I was passing and saw a light. I knew you had band practice, so I thought I'd have a quick look to make sure there weren't any burglars."

Granny Erica looked at him with a puzzled frown. "So you sneak around here in the dark? How did you even get in?"

"I didn't want them to see me. I came in through the back door, so I could catch them red-handed. Looks like they were already gone though."

Erica's gaze wandered from Baudrons and Birtwistle to the kitchen cupboard, which was still open. She seemed to have come to some kind of realisation, because suddenly she relaxed and smiled at him. Only her fingers were still clenched around the case she was holding.

"How fortunate that there are people like you who look after their neighbours," she declared. "How about a cup of tea to say thank you? And then we should call the police. We don't want the burglars trying to break into another home, do we?"

Birtwistle waved dismissively. "I don't think that will be necessary. It was probably a false alarm anyway. There's nothing missing, is there? Maybe you forgot to switch off the light when you left."

Again, the old woman's eyes darted back and forth between his face, his hands and the kitchen cupboard. Birtwistle watched her closely.

After hesitating briefly, she smiled at him. "I'm sure you're right, Andrew. If I go on like this, I'll be proper dotty soon. I'll just make the tea for us then."

She put her case down next to the sofa and went over to the cupboard. She barely hesitated before she grabbed the bag with the Darjeeling and closed the cupboard door.

The old crone must have noticed that he'd pinched the rheumatism tea from her cupboard, Birtwistle thought. She had probably already seen through him—if not, she soon would. In a flash, he grabbed a large, sharp kitchen knife and held it to the old woman's throat.

"I'm sorry, Erica. I didn't mean to harm you, but I can't let you blab. You can thank your nosy grandson that it's come to this."

At first, she kept completely still. But at the mention of her grandson, she perked up. She looked Birtwistle straight in the eye. "I have to admit, I didn't think you could be this ruthless, Andrew. I sometimes wondered why you spent so much time with an old bat like me, but I thought you were harmless."

Birtwistle sneered. "That was the idea."

"But I really should thank Darren. If it hadn't been for him, I would have died unexpectedly one day, just like

Sue Shepherd. At least this way I'll help to get you convicted."

He slowly shook his head. "I don't think so."

In fact, he was afraid she might be proved right. He had panicked when he had grabbed the knife. But if her body was found with stab wounds, they would soon be on his trail. With all the tricks the police have up their sleeves these days, his move could easily backfire.

He wondered if he could get Erica to drink the poisoned tea. Until now, no one had linked the tea to the deaths. To cover his tracks, he simply had to wash the cup afterwards. Or, even better, he could put a cup of plain tea in front of the body, and nobody would be any the wiser. On the other hand, it seemed doubtful that she'd sit quietly and drink tea with him now. Besides, it would take too long for her to die. He would have to keep her from calling for help, while her grandson could barge in any time.

No. He needed a better plan. He had to make sure the police never found her body. Or if they did, that there was no evidence to suggest anything other than a tragic accident. An old woman walking on her own and losing her way. Out in the Highlands, people disappeared all the time, losing their way on lonely mountain paths. Here by the coast, the sea was the most likely killer. The ocean wouldn't mind being held responsible for the unfortunate death of an old lady. One small misstep and she would fall in, never to be seen again. But it mustn't happen too far from the cottage, otherwise questions would be raised.

Fortunately, Birtwistle knew the footpath that passed right behind the Bagshaw house. It was inconspicuous and it seemed plausible that Erica would walk that way.

He wasn't too concerned about her walking cast. The old biddy had a reputation for obstinacy. If she got something into her head, she did it. It would be an arduous journey dragging the old woman along, but it was doable. He snatched her handbag off her and chucked it towards the sofa, missing it by inches.

"We don't want someone trying to locate your mobile when you don't answer, do we?"

Then he grabbed her by the shoulder and steered her towards the back door. Before he left, he switched off the light.

CHAPTER 25

Birtwistle's home stood lonely and dark in its small garden. Greg glared at its locked door, as if it was to blame that they didn't know where its owner was.

Darren craned his neck, but he barely managed to see past Greg's bear-like form. "Did you really expect him to be here?" he asked.

Greg sighed. "No." He stared at the house, pondering. "His car isn't here," he noted.

"The post van?"

"No. That's probably parked at the post office. He's got a white Fiesta."

"And how does that help us?" There was a hint of panic in Darren's voice.

Greg shrugged his shoulders.

"I still don't understand why he'd suddenly go for my grandmother," Darren blurted out. "As far as we know he always used poison."

"Maybe she worked out that it was him. Whatever happened, we need to find her as soon as possible."

"But how?"

"We should probably call the police after all."

Darren nodded. He dug out his phone and dialled the emergency number. After spending quite a long time explaining the situation, he sighed.

"Alright," he said and hung up.

Greg looked at him questioningly.

"They're sending someone, although I'm not sure they believed me. We're to meet them at Granny's home."

Greg mumbled something unintelligible. He started the engine and turned around.

Just before they reached the drive at Granny Erica's cottage, Greg slammed on the brakes. He frowned at a car parked in front of one of the neighbouring houses.

"That could be Birtwistle's car," he said.

"Are you sure?"

"No, but it's a holiday home. It should be empty at this time of year."

Greg got out to have a closer look at the car, leaving the engine of the Corsa running. He was back within the minute.

"Nothing to see there. I could barely feel any warmth from the bonnet but I'm fairly certain it's Birtwistle's."

He got into the car and drove on to Granny Erica's deserted cottage. Janet and Norma were waiting for them at the front door, both looking worried.

"Have you found her?" Norma asked, before Greg and Darren had time to get out of the car.

Greg shook his head and went inside, while Darren quickly recounted what they had done so far. When the other three entered the kitchen, Greg had already grabbed a torch.

"We have to search the area for her," he announced. "Birtwistle's car is parked nearby, so they can't be far." He looked at Darren, who gritted his teeth and nodded. He was afraid of what they might find if Birtwistle had actually attacked his grandmother.

"Yes, please go and find her," Janet agreed. "We'll stay here and wait for the police."

CHAPTER 26

It was dark and windy on the path across the moor. Directly behind the house, trees and large bushes shielded the path, but after only a short distance they gave way to open moorland. During the summer, it was covered in bracken and heather as far as the eye could see.

Birtwistle dragged Erica along by her coat collar. Now that they were out of earshot of the houses, he didn't need to keep threatening her with the knife. Her screams would be futile, and she couldn't run away from him with her cast. Annoyingly though, the stupid thing was hindering her progress more than he had expected and their pace had slowed to a crawl.

"Why, Andrew? Why are you doing this? What did poor Mrs Attwood do to you? Or Sue Shepherd?"

Instead of an answer, he gave her a shove that sent her staggering forwards, arms flailing. He had no intention of getting involved in a conversation with her. That would only make the end harder for both of them.

In fact, doubts had been creeping up on him since they had got out here. Giving the old ladies poisoned tea they would drink by themselves was one thing. Murdering someone with your own hands was quite another.

You have no choice, his inner voice reminded him. It's basically self-defence. The old biddy knows too much. If you let her go now, you'll spend the rest of your days in prison.

That was true, even if he dreaded killing her.

After a seemingly endless walk and several breaks to allow the whinging old woman to rest, they were within a couple of hundred yards of the cliffs. That's where he wanted to go. During the day it would have been a walk of barely fifteen minutes, but in the dark it was much more difficult to follow the narrow path, especially with the old woman's cast.

Birtwistle had repeatedly cursed himself for not simply taking the car. But somebody might have seen him with Mrs Bagshaw and he definitely didn't want any fibres from her clothes ending up in his car. Small things like that could be his undoing, as he knew well from watching crime programs on TV.

The moon still hadn't risen. Despite the darkness, Birtwistle had no intention of using his torch, which would make their position visible from afar. All they could do in the sparse light was to try to make out the dark soil of the path between the slightly brighter grass and bracken. They stumbled again and again, but Birtwistle didn't allow old Mrs Bagshaw to slow down any more.

Eventually they reached the point where the footpath turned up the cliffs. It went north here, towards the Ganavan Maze, which was little more than a pile of small rocks that somebody had arranged into a simple circular maze. Even in summer it wasn't particularly impressive. Children might get a few minutes entertainment out of following the paths until the grass swallowed the maze in June.

Birtwistle stopped for a moment. The sea glittered faintly in the starlight. Further out, he could see the dark outline of Lismore Island. A few scattered lights indicated that the world didn't end there. A stiff breeze was blowing in his face and tugging on his jacket. A proper storm would be better, it occurred to him, but this would have to do.

After another couple of hundred yards, they reached the viewpoint. The cliffs here dropped at least a hundred feet to the sea. That didn't sound like much, but a person falling off might as well jump from the tenth floor of a tower block. And below there wasn't just water, but sharp rocks breaking the waves into white foaming spray.

"Stop!" Birtwistle ordered as they reached the highest point.

Erica sank to the ground, exhausted.

That didn't bother him for the moment. He moved the kitchen knife to his left hand and fumbled in his pocket with his right. He pulled out the tea tin he had taken from Erica's kitchen.

"The last evidence," he muttered.

He opened the tin and poured its contents into the wind. When it was empty, he hurled the tin into the sea.

"Now it's your turn."

The old woman looked up at him pleadingly. "Andrew, please, this won't help you. I'm sure you don't really want to do this."

Birtwistle hesitated briefly. There is no more evidence, his conscience whispered. What could possibly happen? Nobody can prove that you had anything to do with the death of Sue Shepherd or any of the other victims.

Then a second, harder voice took over. What about the kidnapping? You should've just grabbed the tin and got out. Now it's too late. You better deal with her right here. This is your only chance.

He shook his head to rid himself of those thoughts. Then he stepped towards the old woman sitting on the ground.

CHAPTER 27

With the dancing light of the torch showing him the way, Darren ran along the narrow footpath leading to the sea. Greg was convinced they had gone this way because in the other direction you soon reached the main road.

"If they are on this path, you might still be able to catch up with them." Greg's words were echoing in his head as he stumbled through the darkness. The chances of finding his grandmother out here might be slim, but at least Greg's advice gave him something to do. Anything was better than staying in his Granny's home with Janet and Norma having nothing to do but to wait and to worry.

Again and again, he flashed the beam of the torch across the moorland to see if they had left the path somewhere. But it was no more than a reflex that he didn't put much hope in. For one thing, Birtwistle was unlikely to leave the path for the slow-going rough ground, and for another, Darren had hardly any chance of spotting them even if they were out there. So he hoped they were still somewhere along the path.

Meanwhile, Greg took the car to Ganavan Sands. He planned to walk the path along the sea and meet up with Darren where his path met the one coming from Granny Erica's home. He would also alert Pete at the pub, although he could only tell him that Erica Bagshaw was missing, possibly on the moors. Explaining their suspicions against Andrew Birtwistle would take too long.

Better they got some extra pairs of eyes out into the night as soon as possible.

Darren was panting. The uneven path, the tension and his pace were starting to take their toll. As was his lack of fitness. Maybe he should have exercised occasionally. Fell running might be a popular hobby in rural Scotland, but Darren had always been suspicious of those obsessed runners. Besides, it wasn't really a hobby for the city boy he had become in the last few years. Who could have foreseen that he would have to deal with a situation like this?

The moon rose over the hills to the east, suddenly bathing the landscape in pale yellow light. Darren slowed his pace to look around. He switched off his torch when he realised that its bright beam interfered with his ability to see in the still faint light of the moon.

Scanning the landscape, he saw nothing—neither on the open moor to his right nor on the path ahead. There was a fence to the left, the nearest houses not far behind. If Birtwistle was hiding there for some reason, Darren had no chance of finding him.

Groaning, he set off at a trot again. When he reached the shore, he turned right towards the viewpoint. Greg would be searching the area to the left. He should get here from the Ganavan Sands car park in a few minutes. The wind, which never really died down at the shore, had picked up and was tugging at his jacket and hair.

Darren was so short of breath that he had to walk up the cliff to the viewpoint. He also wondered what he should do if he actually met Birtwistle. It certainly wouldn't help if all he could do was gasp for air.

When he had nearly reached the top, Darren sensed someone coming towards him. He could just make out a faint silhouette moving in the shadows of the bushes that grew up here. Was it Birtwistle?

Darren stopped. Should he hide? What if the postman was armed? Why hadn't he thought about what he would do if he found Birtwistle and his grandmother? Darren dithered. Whoever it was didn't seem to have noticed him, as they continued cautiously and unhurried down the path.

When they stepped out of the shadows, Darren realised how small the figure was. In the moonlight, he saw white hair floating above a dark coat like a will-o'-the-wisp.

"Hello?"

The person flinched and turned to hobble back up the path.

"Granny Erica! It's me, Darren!" He switched on the torch to light up his face.

"Darren? What are you doing out here?" His grandmother sounded surprised, but also incredibly relieved.

CHAPTER 28

"How did you escape?" the policewoman asked.

They were sitting around the table in Granny Erica's cottage. Each of them had a steaming cup of tea with plenty of sugar. Proper tea, of course, because they would be very suspicious of herbal tea for the foreseeable future.

Granny Erica shook her head in amazement. "To be honest, I'm not quite sure what happened. He was just about to kill me, when the moon came up. Maybe the sudden light blinded him. At least that's how it seemed to me. His eyes went wide and he held up his hands as if to ward off the moonlight. When he took a step backwards he stumbled. I saw his arms flailing, then he was gone. The edge of the cliff had been right behind him. He fell before I could do anything."

It hadn't been quite like that, Darren knew, even though it probably was exactly what his grandmother had seen. But Grandpa Alan had told a different story. His ghostly face had been floating over her shoulder like a happy balloon when Darren hugged her tightly, relieved to find her unharmed.

The ghost had been the one who had scared the wits out of Birtwistle by appearing right out of his wife's body, screaming and howling like a banshee. He had been utterly surprised that the murderous postman had been able to see him. Then again, maybe he hadn't. But he must have sensed enough of the ghost's blind fury to feel terrified.

The mere fact that Grandpa Alan had been able to follow them all the way to the cliffs was impressive. Maybe it had been his desperation, or his anger at himself that gave him the strength to leave the house. He believed he should have noticed that something wasn't right with the postman.

Darren had been filled in on the events out on the cliff by an exhilarated ghost while he slowly and carefully escorted his grandmother to the car park at Ganavan Sands.

Fortunately, everything had turned out well in the end. At least for Granny Erica. They didn't know what had happened to Andrew Birtwistle after he had lost his footing. Erica had heard him screaming for a while after the accident, so he obviously hadn't drowned immediately. But when Greg, Pete and some men from the pub searched the cliff side for Birtwistle a short time later, there was no sign of him. They assumed he had been washed into the sea. However, an extensive search by police and coastguard would have to wait until daybreak. As the wind strengthened into a gale, it was too dangerous out there now.

Meanwhile, Darren and his grandmother told the policewoman everything they had found out about Andrew Birtwistle and his schemes. Much of it was conjecture, but it raised enough questions to warrant investigation.

Finding evidence for the postman's murders was going to be difficult after he had poured the last of the poisoned tea into the wind. Nevertheless, he wouldn't get away scot-free if they caught him alive. Threatening and kidnapping Erica Bagshaw would be enough for a charge and prison sentence in any case.

CHAPTER 29

Two days had passed since Granny Erica's ordeal. Darren was sitting under the big tree in the garden of Rose Cottage, waiting for nightfall. To avoid being noticed by the Stickles next door, he had parked down the road and quietly walked over.

As he watched the sun slowly disappear behind the horizon, he thought about what had happened.

His grandmother had weathered her abduction and the night-time trip across the moors surprisingly well. She had been treated for hypothermia and shock that night, drinking lots of sweet tea and having long conversations with him and the police. And, of course, everyone had had a dram or two of the Scottish water of life, *uisge beatha*. Now Granny Erica just needed some time to recover from her exhaustion.

By breakfast the next morning, which Darren prepared for once, she was almost back to her usual self. She ordered her grandson around the kitchen so much that he wished he could have put her back to bed.

Only her doctor at the hospital wasn't happy with her. That was hardly surprising. Her walking cast was meant for moving about at home and maybe visiting friends, not for hikes across the moors. Nevertheless, after he had examined her foot and given her an anti-inflammatory injection as a precaution, he seemed convinced that no lasting damage had been done.

Andrew Birtwistle had survived his fall. The police apprehended him the next morning when he was trying to sneak into his home, looking dirty and dishevelled. Apparently he just wanted to pack and then get away to Europe or some other place where he could live off the money he had earned from his poisonings. But thanks to Granny Erica's testimony, that plan went nowhere. He was arrested and taken to the police station in Oban for questioning.

Meanwhile, an investigation regarding the suspected series of murders in and around Ganavan had been set up. Katie Beales and Darren's grandmother had told the police everything they knew. But without the poisoned tea or expert statements from doctors regarding the presumed victims it would be difficult to prove Birtwistle's crimes. Of course they would try, but as most of the victims had been buried or even cremated months ago, it could take a long time to get conclusive evidence.

Libby Whatmough voluntarily shared her information with the police. She told them about her agreement with the postie to hand out her flyers and business cards to likely clients. Of course she had paid him for the houses he had sent her way, she admitted. But how was she to know that the couple of thousand pounds he got each time would be an incentive for him to become a serial killer? She felt awful about the whole affair.

When Aunt Janet learnt that the postman had killed his victims with poisoned rheumatism tea, she was stupefied. She, too, had got one of his pretty tea tins and even though she had turned up her nose at this Christmas present in front of the others, she had been delighted. On several cold days since then, she had thought about brewing herself a cup. Fortunately, something always came up.

However, an analysis of her tea in the police laboratory showed it was harmless. Just ordinary rheumatism tea from the shop in Oban. Janet, who had thought she had narrowly escaped death, was almost disappointed.

"It seems Andrew had no hope of making money from your home. Even with you gone, he would have needed something stronger than tea to get rid of all your brood," Norma observed. She had never got a present from Andrew Birtwistle. Whether it was because she was Libby's aunt, or because he simply didn't like her, was anyone's guess.

The afternoon after Birtwistle's arrest, Darren remembered something: Maggie—or more to the point, the tea she had taken from Mrs Attwood's house. That, too, had been a tin of rheumatism tea from Argyll Herbs and Teas, just like his grandmother's. Then he remembered how curious Birtwistle had been about the rubbish that Darren had removed from the house.

Of course, Maggie was not happy that Darren had told the police about the pilfered tea. If she got a reputation for stealing from the houses she worked in, she would struggle to hold on to her job. Although obviously it would be much worse if she or someone close to her had been poisoned with the tea.

The lab analysis later showed that the tea did indeed contain a large amount of the toxins typical for lily of the valley. Half a cup would suffice to cause serious symptoms of poisoning. More would be fatal.

Step by step the story came to light, although many questions remained.

Darren wasn't going to tell all of this to Tony Shepherd the ghost, just enough to fulfil his promise to find out why his wife had died. Obviously, this wouldn't change anything for Sue now. Proving that Birtwistle was guilty of her death wouldn't help her. There was, however, some consolation for her husband. Through his persistence, a series of murders had been discovered that had claimed the lives of far too many elderly people. The murderer would be punished, and Sue and Tony could finally rest in peace.

Darren had consulted his grandfather the night before about the best way to help the ghost. As darkness fell, Tony appeared in the shadow of a rose bush. He seemed restless and anxious, but when he saw Darren smiling, he stopped fidgeting.

It took Darren more than half an hour to tell Tony about the events of the last few days. When he had finished, the ghost breathed a sigh of relief. They sat under the tree together and Tony told him about his wife. How they had met and fallen in love and about their life together. When the moon rose, there was nothing more to say.

Darren smiled at Tony. "Please give her my regards. I would have loved to meet her."

Tony nodded. "I'm sure she'd have liked that."

He raised his hand in farewell—and disappeared.

EPILOGUE

"Thank you, Mrs Bagshaw. Your cranachan was wonderful, just like everything else, but I really can't eat any more." Katie leaned back and carefully placed a hand on her tummy.

Darren could sympathise. He too had eaten far more than was good for him. But his grandmother had put so much effort into the meal that he just couldn't resist.

Granny Erica beamed with pleasure. "Very well. I'll just make you a coffee before I'm off to band practice."

That got Darren to his feet, even though he immediately regretted getting up with so much vigour, as his full stomach ached with every move. "Thanks Granny, but I'll make the coffee."

She looked at him amused. "Suit yourself. By the way, I got you an espresso maker."

"You have?" Delighted, Darren looked around. "Where is it?"

"In the cupboard, of course." She picked up her bagpipes and headed for the door. "Have fun then, you two. And don't do anything I wouldn't do." She winked at Darren before grabbing her umbrella and closing the door behind her.

"Of course not," he mumbled, wondering what exactly his grandmother would *not* do. He couldn't think of anything.

"Shall I help you?" Katie asked, getting up from the table too. She opened the cupboard where the coffee was kept and laughed.

"Do you think this is what she meant by an espresso maker?" She showed him an antique-looking stovetop moka pot.

Darren groaned. "I expect she did. Sorry about that."

"Don't worry, you can make excellent coffee with one of these." Katie quickly filled it with water and ground coffee and put it on the stove.

When he took the first sip a few minutes later, Darren had to agree with her. It was the best coffee he'd ever had at House Bagshaw.

"How are you doing at the hospital since all this happened?" he asked. He hadn't wanted to bring up Birtwistle while his grandmother was there.

Katie shrugged. "It's okay, I guess. A few of the doctors are still miffed because they think I challenged their authority." She rolled her eyes. "But most of the others are glad. Did I tell you that I got an official commendation from management last week?"

Darren smiled. "Congratulations!"

"Thank you." She traced the rim of her coffee cup thoughtfully. "I've been thinking about going to medical school. I could go to Edinburgh." She looked at Darren expectantly.

"Uh-huh." He sipped from his coffee.

Katie sighed. "On the other hand, I like Oban. I like my job and I'm good at it, and most of my family live here too."

"I see." Darren nodded.

Katie huffed impatiently. "That's all you've got to say about this?"

He sighed. "Of course I'm happy for you, whatever you decide. I'm sure it would be great to be in Edinburgh together, but right now I don't even know if I want to go back myself. I don't have a job there, and my flatmate has thrown me out. On the other hand, Libby has also told me she's letting me go."

Katie's eyes widened. "What? Why?"

Darren shrugged. "She didn't literally say that it was because of the Birtwistle affair, but I still think it was. It's certainly affected her business. She told me she won't need another cleaner this summer. Maggie can handle it."

As if to underline the hopelessness of his situation, it was getting even darker outside. It had been raining all afternoon, but now it was pouring down as if someone wanted to wash Ganavan off the map.

Katie looked at him sympathetically. "What are you going to do now?"

Darren raised his hands helplessly. "I don't know." Suddenly he noticed his grandfather standing in the dark corner behind Katie. He was smiling. "I guess I'll just stay here for now. There's something I need to see to. While I'm at it I might as well look for a new job in Oban. The tourist season is starting, so I suppose it won't be too hard to find something—you'll spend the summer here as well, won't you? Even if you do want to become a doctor, your courses won't start until autumn anyway, so you still have some time to decide. We could see each other on your days off, you know."

Katie smiled. "You're right. That sounds great. If you want, I can help you find a job. I know someone who works in one of the backpacker hostels. It's right in the centre of Oban. So we could easily walk over to Markie Dans in the evenings."

"Let's do that." Darren smiled broadly.

Maybe I'll even get a chance to visit that former church in Benderloch again, he thought. I really have to ask Grandpa Alan whether poltergeists are real.

DEAR READER

I hope you enjoyed Darren Bagshaw's first case. There are more to come.

I'm a great admirer of the Scottish west coast, the Highlands and Islands. However, I'm not a local, and although I've done my best, there will be errors and misrepresentations, as well as changes made for the sake of the plot. I hope those of you who know Oban and the surrounding area will forgive me.

All the characters and some of the places like the Haunted House Pub, Granny Erica's home and Argyll Herbs and Teas are figments of my imagination.

If you like, you can visit some of the other places though. I very much liked Markie Dans, the pub in Oban. But you can also visit Ganavan Sands, walk up to McCaig's Tower on Battery Hill or enjoy the scenic trip on the ferry to Mull.

For a delicious Scottish dessert, try Granny Erica's recipe for

Scottish Cranachan (Serves 8)
Cranachan is a Scottish dessert classic, preferably served in June when raspberries are plentiful. The classic Cranachan recipe calls for dry toasted oats. But I prefer this version giving them some extra flavour and crunch.

For the caramelised oats put 100g (or 4 oz) of rolled oats, 100g (or 4 oz) of brown sugar and a knob of butter in a frying pan and stir over high heat for a few minutes until they are toasted and crunchy. Take care not to burn them. Set aside to cool.

Then whip 500ml (or 1 pint) of double cream (or heavy cream) to stiff peaks.

Add 3 tablespoons of whisky to the cream. I like to use a lighter and fruitier variety like Glenmorangie or a whisky from Speyside, but of course that's up to your own taste. Now add about two thirds of the cooled oats and about 300g (10 oz) of raspberries (keep some more for garnishing). Stir until combined, but try to keep the raspberries fairly whole. Taste the mix and add sugar or more whisky if you like.

Spoon into dessert glasses and sprinkle the rest of the crunchy oats over the top. Add raspberries and a little heather honey for garnish.

Enjoy!

(Recipe inspired by Mary Berry's Cranachan)

If you enjoyed this book, consider leaving a review or rating on the platform where you bought it, or share it with friends who might also enjoy it. You can also support me by purchasing a copy for yourself or as a gift.

Want to know more about me or my books?
Follow me on Instagram @ima.ahorn_writes for updates on my current projects.

Darren's next case "The Death of a Ghost Hunter" will be available in 2026.

Printed in Dunstable, United Kingdom